WALKING VANILLA

WALKING VANILLA
AN ORAL NOVEL TO BE DANCED TO
by
SUSAN EFROS

Waterfall Press
1357 Hopkins Street
Berkeley, CA 94702

Three thousand copies of this book
were printed in November, 1978 by
Fremont Litho. Typography by
Ann Flanagan. Assembly by Jane
Bernard. Cover design by
Georgia Oliva.

Dedication:

This novel is officially dedicated to:

Joan Levinson, Michael Poniatowski, Rosalie Cassell, Shannon O'Brien, Diane Rusnak, Wendy Guggenheim, Kathy Barry, Toni Vian, Mikkel Aaland, Bob Adler, Betty McAfee, David Matson, Liz Zima, Marcia Perlstein, Barbara Zoloth, Gloria Bosque, Oralee Wachter, Barbara Custer, Ann Flanagan, Jane Bernard, Jackie Dennis, the Women of the Women's Performing Arts Center, The Balance Point, The Walnut House Family Nuts, and a special Wyomian, Roz Cochran, for their practical assistance, emotional support, massages and pot luck suppers.

Preface

"All the characters in this novel are good friends of mine."

The Author

Walking Vanilla Characters

BRETT STARR	28 year old Leo Woman
JACOB MOSCOVITZ	28 year old Aries Man
ANNIE OAKHURST	28 year old Scorpio Feminist
FENMARIAN	An Androgenous Flea (Aquarius)
TUNA MELITTA	The Cat (Cancer)
WALKING VANILLA	A Concept
BUDDY	A Professional White Male (Capricorn)
AUTHOR	The Narrator (Pisces)
BARTON AND GLORIA STARR	Brett's Mother and Father
SY AND VY MOSCOVITZ	Jacob's Mother and Father
AN ANONYMOUS CALLER	A. C.
A STUDENT	Nameless

1 THIS IS THE STORY of a relationship that breaks apart in three days, a fairly long affair considering the times. it lasts all the way from Tuesday until Friday. the two people seriously cohabitate, share their possessions, meals, bodies, thoughts, dreams, futures and toothpaste during this period.

It is very, very heavy.

When they break up over irreconcilable differences, she takes the leftover croissants, and he takes the remains of a half pound bag of french roast coffee, jointly purchased at Peet's Coffee Tea and Spices Shop, when they still had no idea they were incompatible.

Her name is Brett.

His name is Jacob.

They are pretty nice people, not great, but pretty nice.

She thinks: i thought it might last a month or two, at least.

He thinks: i knew it wouldn't last.

She thinks: he was really good in bed, but not much to talk to.

He thinks: she wasn't so hot in bed, but it was great to have company.

You can see already why they didn't last.

She thinks: i have fat thighs.

He thinks: my arms are not muscular enough.

She thinks: he has a great body!

He thinks: she has a great body!

They both have misconceived perceptions of their body image. they are both a little neurotic; isn't everybody?

They both think: it was her (his) fault.

We all know everything, especially love, is constantly in flux, even if we never get used to it. Walking Vanilla melting all over concrete examples.

2 IN SEARCH OF SOMETHING richer is always chapter two. something substantial: a cafeteria of love. something fresh instead of soggy. a hofbrau of the heart. it only happens once in a lifetime, or at the movies, or to friends, or in novels, romantic sonnets and dreams. night after night, Brett's and Jacob's parents whispered of charming princes and princesses at bedtime. no wonder these two are still seeking love, even after all the pain. their parents were as persistent and effective as foreign language tapes. so from very early childhood, romantic love is ingrained in Brett and Jacob as a second language. it is a deep, deep habit within them. they are like pieces of wood with a variety of emotional carvings. fear is deeply ingrained along with love. it is a tough battle between the grains.

Sometimes, Brett and Jacob turn their backs on each other and say things like "why bother" and "nothing ever works." i don't pay attention to them when they speak this way, though i understand what they mean.

Still, i am going to write this novel, with or without their cooperation. i'm not going to let their cynical grains slow me down.

Our generation changed a lot of things, but it didn't eliminate the problem of survival. even artists need money, food and bandaids; essentials are universal. our generation eliminated a lot of unnecessary baggage, but not the uni-

versal bag of fear and survival. there certainly is an immense amount of mania, meditation and depression in the
current air, as well as overeating and jogging. it's a pretty
extreme time. everyone i know and even people i don't
know are pretty weird. what do you think?

PERSONALLY, i should be happier than i am.

SOCIALLY, i am happier than several people i know.

HISTORICALLY, i have no idea.

COSMICALLY, this is the age of "what the fuck is
going on?"

The characters in my novel can't sit still. neither can i.
neither can you. hardly any of us are stationary. we're
movers. this is a time when people are in a great hurry. i
wonder why? where is everyone going right now, i ask myself? hey you, where are you rushing off to? do you have
time to read this novel? probably not. (even if it's a novel-
ette?)

Oh well. Brett and Jacob aren't practical anyway. they
were just made up to fill in the blanks. a novel has to have
characters, right? and the blanks have to be filled in. characters have to have astrological signs, these days anyway.
Brett is a Leo and Jacob is an Aries. you'll find out everybody else's sign as we move along. be patient. the author
will tell you everything if you trust her.

3   the author is making
    this up
    she is making
    herself up
    in the mirror
    she is changing
    the form
    her mind
    writing a poem
    instead
    of the novel
    see how fickle
    a novelist
    is unexpectedly

things do
change/will
even the line
on the page
has altered dramatically
since we began this
venture into
the brain which will
transform you
if you let it
enter
whoever
you are
pretending
to be.

BUT WE ARE REAL. Brett is real. she does feel pain. a warm hand slipped into her cold hand on a winter's night. a brush combing her long, ash blonde hair. a friendship piercing her heart. a piece of danish pastry stuck, for example, in her throat.

4 IF YOU FEEL like a failure, WALK WITH VANILLA. walk with this novel all over your life. don't get stuck, frozen to your pain. don't be a big block of ice, sitting on a couch stuck to a bag of greasy pastry contemplating suicide. it's not healthy. besides, it will upset your friends. Walking Vanilla is an alternative. this is not propaganda for a big, rip-off organization. it is simply universal grassroots common sense. it's pretty friendly stuff.

GREASY PASTRY IS A UNIVERSAL PERVERSITY. sugar makes you weird. the PAVLOVIAN SUGAR RESPONSE. ring. ring. the buzzer for ice cream and pastry go off. the roller coaster of civilization goes up and down. up and down. we go with sugar/coffee/pasta and booze. nothing gets going when you're eating neurotically.

When Brett and Jacob break up, they sit on separate couches in separate apartments, stuffing themselves with separate bags of greasy pastry, cigarettes and wine. it's a rotten situation to get oneself into, and a sticky place to get out of. it's like cement. don't you get stuck like Brett and Jacob thinking stuck thoughts like "nothing works," and "i'm defeated." if you break up with someone, or lose a high paying job, quickly, put on your hiking boots, that's right. tie the laces and get up, get up and WALK WITH VANILLA.

It is not so easy to walk with vanilla as the author thinks it is. trust me. i know. i've tried.

This is the story that pops up like toast. when it's done it will walk right off the page. the artist has the prerogative to walk right off the page when words become too much or too little.

5   Brett: what are you doing, Jacob?
     Jacob: i'm counting my pennies.
     Brett: do you have enough for a bottle of wine?
     Jacob: barely enough for laundry detergent. it's depressing. when will it end, Brett? concentrating on survival gives me a headache. i want to create. i want to quit my lousy job at the radio station. i want you to quit your lousy job at the bakery. we deserve more than soap suds.
     Brett: things will change, Jacob. don't despair. we're still young.
     Jacob: we're twenty-eight.
     Brett: well, that's young.
     Jacob: today, it feels old.
     Brett: ah hon. you'll see. you'll feel a lot younger when you get into some clean clothes, when you get those greasy overalls off. don't you think so?
     Jacob: yeah, i suppose. i am pretty filthy after working under the car all day.
     Brett: sure. i think grease has got you down.
                                    . . .
You can't make a living as an artist. only 3 percent of all living writers make a living writing. the other 97 percent keep trying or are dead. nobody knows who the 3 percent are. a number of investigators, including myself, think they are made up.

Brett and Jacob are struggling young artists. they are made up, so they don't count in the statistics. Brett is a female artist who wants to be with a man. Jacob is a male artist who wants to be with a woman; they are traditional in certain respects. they want to be with each other. they don't get along. they aren't even attracted to each other (anymore). they are both thinking: see. not only am i a poor, struggling artist with dirty laundry, but i just fell out of love as well.

Life is not easy. in fact, is is often quite filthy.

Simultaneously, Brett and Jacob are thinking: maybe we should try again. maybe it's time to COMPROMISE. just a little? maybe we have more in common than we imagine. we make life too difficult for ourselves by being so idealistic and rash. we demand too much. there is more to life than passion and excitement. there's security and communication and working things out. there's putting our heads and finances together. the age old problem of money. bills encroaching like an army. they'd like to go AWOL.

Brett and Jacob, two young clever artists, with everything in life ahead of them, are thinking: well, we do have a lot in common. we do have the french roast coffee, for example, and some other things too. they can't recall at the moment what other things, but they are certain there are things. oh yes, they are both artists and struggling and horny and afraid of being alone for the winter.

Even struggling young artists think bourgeoise thoughts, especially in the winter. they think about forced-air heating, blue cross insurance and leather coats. they are both trying hard to believe in cliches and early childhood tapes. they are both pretty smart cookies with college degrees and upper middle class backgrounds, so they have a tough job on their hands.

They are both thinking: he(she) could sure be a lot worse. he (she) is a lot better than a lot of men (women) i know. she (he) is nice to be with in the dark (sunshine). my friends seem affirmative. that's something. not much, but a consideration. she (he) has talent and brains and a respect-

6

able body. it's not everything but it does impress a lot of people at parties. it also replaces electric blankets, which neither character can afford.

Brett and Jacob are thinking these common, everyday thoughts while walking on different streets in their hiking boots on different sidewalks. they are walking farther and farther away from each other without knowing it. i know it because i am watching them from my helicopter. you didnt know i had a helicopter, did you? well, it's a new fact of the novel that just popped up. i can see the characters clearly from here, and neither of them is walking with vanilla. they are thinking their private, special, made up lies, and not believing a single word. it's typical. it's perfectly normal.

Jacob: i've got enough to think about without worrying about a tenuous relationship with a moody blonde.

Brett: he's touchy. but together we can be strong. together we can overcome circumstances/temperaments/weather conditions. i think we can? i feel an urge to combine my art work with an intimate relationship. maybe it's because i'm entering my saturn return astrologically. combining with Jacob might be a higher form of my personal development. i hope our chemistry doesn't mess us up.

Jacob: i bet she messes up my car with cigarette butts. she has no respect for machinery. and she drinks a lot. who can afford her bad habits? not me. i'm barely able to pay the rent.

Brett: why can't i be attracted to men with a little working capital? is it my karma to fall in love with poverty cases?

However, dear readers, there is no need to feel sorry for our tragic characters. they are only characters. made-up words. keep that in mind, just in case anyone bleeds profusely, swallows poison, collapses in the theater, or gets evicted from their apartment. remember they are harmless words. scratched in or out with a flick of the wrist/the pen/the murderer/me.

6 IT'S NICE to have a good book to read. but don't take too many along when you travel. you won't see. there are better times to read a novel than when on the go, on

the Isle of Capri, for instance. better times to get outside yourself than in Honolulu. so, if you are in Spain right now or somewhere equally beautiful, put this novel down. read it later. i won't be offended and neither will my characters. i'll explain it to them; we are very close.

But, on the other hand, if you are stuck in the house with three or more snot-nosed kids and NO ESCAPE, well it would be a fine time to bury your head in this novel, any novel for that matter. better than burying your fingers in dirty dishes, certainly.

Brett and Jacob can wait. so pick the appropriate time to get involved in their lives. i did. i picked Christmas vacation. i am using Brett and Jacob to avoid the holidays. it's pretty sneaky. people say "come to the party! drink this and taste that." i say "i can't. i'm too busy writing a novel." i am avoiding egg nog and lonely men with a long, prose piece.

Brett and Jacob are pretty miserable in most respects. isn't that COMFORTING? they are suffering from a common disease which brought them together in the same novel: FEAR. additionally, they both have advanced complications of anxiety and repressed anger. they are your average, everyday, pretty nice but not great americans, living in Berkeley, freaking out and also doing a lot of normal things like the laundry. right now, in fact, they are doing some normal things. listen:

Brett: yes Jacob. i've just got to do the laundry. i haven't any towels left, and you haven't any pants left, except those greasy ones you have on.

Jacob: sure you don't need company?

Brett: no. not really. i'll just bring a book along. i know you want to finish up on the car.

Jacob: how long do you think you'll be?

Brett: well, let's see. half an hour for wash. forty-five minutes for dry. i guess an hour and a half to be on the safe side.

Jacob: well listen, hon. i'll work on the car and come by the laundromat. we'll go out for a pizza and beer, my treat. what do you say?

Brett: sounds great, i'll be starving by then. but hey, where are you going to get the money?

Jacob: i think i can sell a few books at Moe's.

Brett: oh hon. are you sure you want to do that?

Jacob: of course. it will lighten my load. anyway, i'm starving too. it's seven now. i'll meet you at 8:30. o.k.?

Brett: (affectionately) perfect. hey grease monkey, don't forget to wash your hands before handling the goods.

They laugh in charming unison. Jacob kisses Brett affectionately.

Jacob: right! and don't you forget to wash the clothes with soap. here. hold onto the Tide; it's our last major investment for the week. see ya soon.

. . .

It's nice to be outside. yourself. to walk through neurosis/the laundromat/the great outdoors. to stroll with vanilla through streets/books/flesh/forests. to taste the sweet possibilities on your tongue. the fierce desire to love immensely with vanilla.

Sway in the breeze. hold your head up high and clean and white, billowing like sails in the afternoon wind. do not think: i am crazy. do not think: i am ugly. do not think: why am i reading this novel? think instead: i am snapping my fingers and overcoming everything, even my birth trauma with a good attitude. this is your novel/movie. the cameras are all pointed in your direction. the screen is stretched across a huge immaculate vanilla desert/universe. you are large, larger than life. you are more than enough. this is your chapter. do with it as you please. the next five lines can be filled in, or left blank for the purpose of silence. regardless, get involved/with something. it's better than greasy pastry.

_____

_____

_____

7   LATER AT THE LAUNDROMAT, our tale continues to spin, and our characters continue ironing things out.

Brett: damn it, Jacob! it's 9:20. where have you been?

Jacob: listen, Brett. i'm getting sick and tired of you pinning me down to the minute. what do you think i am, a machine?

Brett: just about! i've been ready since 8:15. do you think i enjoy hanging out in this stupid laundromat?

Jacob: you said 8:30.

Brett: *you* said 8:30.

Jacob: we both said 8:30. so what! Jesus Christ. all we ever do is argue. (Jacob paces the cold, damp floor, folding and unfolding his agitated arms.) i had to finish putting the manifold back on, didn't i? i had to go up to crummy Telegraph Avenue and sell books, didn't i?

Brett (smugly): did you?

Jacob: (disgusted): do you want to get a pizza or not? i'm starving, i've worked hard. i'm fed up! i'm going anyway. so make up your mind.

Brett (turning her back on him, spinning away from his skinny arm with a quick cold shoulder): skip it. just skip the whole thing. go play with your car! take it out for a damn pizza.

Jacob: fine with me. treats me better. it's a hell of a lot simpler!

Brett (flatly): so are you.

Brett gathers the clean laundry in her arms and exits cooly. she is whistling as if everything were perfectly fine, when, in fact, everything is thoroughly rotten. Jacob lights a cigarette, inhales deeply, shrugs his shoulders and exits whistling the same old tune. they are both nonchalant and miserable, and off key; it's perfectly normal.

Everyone wants to be themselves, be at ease, and get along. but it seems impossible for any extended period of time. it's a big mess. a pile of dirty laundry, a matrix of personalities crossing and overlapping in bizarre patterns and configurations. the human condition spinning and spinning and intertwining in knots.

Everyone keeps trying to get clean. to get straight. to untangle themselves. everyone hopes against hope that they will iron out their difficulties and fall warmly in love.

. . .

It's lonely inside an empty belly. food does not fill the hunger for laughter.

. . .

Brett looks deeply into Jacob's blue eyes at the corner drugstore, and does not recognize him. he recognizes her but pretends not to. someone else, myself, recognizes both of them and knows they are avoiding each other with their sharpest avoidance tools. i am writing this down as a record of their mutual deceit. i could put it on a tape recorder, video or celluloid and it would be the same story, the same old story.

You see, they did care. once, briefly, they looked out of the corner of burning eyes at the corner cafe in order to recognize each other, they looked very deeply into blue and green eyes. though they never have truly recognized each other's motives. i invented them both so i know their emotions. yes, they did love each other from tuesday until friday. they both have perfect vision so they could see what they were doing. neither wears glasses. they were very real: three-dimensional for three days. they were crystal clear. then they shattered. i'm putting it in print so that people, especially Brett and Jacob, won't be able to deny it later on. like many couples, they broke up in a laundromat. proving once again that. . . eyesight and vision are not the same thing.

8 Brett: the author of this novel is obviously a liar, well an exaggerator anyway. she is pretending i am in love with Jacob. of course, it's a lie. i can't imagine loving a greasy jerk like that. true, i did sleep with him, once or twice, and it wasn't so bad, but love? a deep meaningful relationship? poo.

Jacob: the author of this novel is mistaken. i wouldn't call her a liar, actually. i'd just say she's a little dizzy, if you know what i mean. anyway, i am the one who got the left-over croissants and Brett took the French roast coffee, that bitch. Brett always has to get her way! she's a spoiled Leo. you know the type. and i never thought much of her con-versation either. as far as i'm concerned, the whole thing's been blown way out of proportion by the author, who wears contact lenses. my trip with Brett was not nearly as heavy or deep as envisioned by the creator of this fiction. she overdramatizes and overscrutinizes; so beware. still, i must add that she is a friend of mine, and does mean well. also, i do recommend this book to children of all ages. it may be full of lies and distortions but it's compassionate, nevertheless.

. . .

INTRODUCING ANNIE, who's taking time out from her brilliant, diligent research to give us some educated guesses. Annie is working towards her Ph.D. in Women's History. she works harder than anyone else in this novel, except, perhaps, the novelist.

Annie: both Brett and Jacob have limited vision. they are attached to each other which, combined with their in-herent tunnel vision, is just about fatal when it comes to foresight. it's a lot more serious than myopia. Brett isn't ready to let go of her near-blindness yet, but i'm working on her. occasionally, i play detective in this novel, that is why i am wearing this trench coat and sunglasses. i'm not sure if i'll do much good, but what are sisters for? to try harder. to work towards unification. to change *his* story into *her* story. Brett needs my advice now, even if she doesn't realize it yet. but first i have to get to the library and do my required research for the afternoon. otherwise, i'll feel like shit.

9 WELL,
how do you like it so far?

10 WHICH PART of your body is most hungry for touch? is it your lips or an elbow, per chance? maybe a knee? it's possible. find that part of your body by trial and error. touch it yourself. touch it some more. indulge it. it's better than nothing.

Brett often touches her thighs. Jacob touches his forehead. almost everyone touches their crotch. if life seems absurd and colorless and the holiday season is drawing near, and nobody is touching your knee, buy a houseplant for insurance, or long underwear or an esalen-style massage. don't buy a half gallon of ice cream. why? o.k., buy it if you really want to.

This is a chapter about people being extraordinarily hard on themselves. it covers a lot of territory. miles and miles and miles of it.

Brett thinks she is a failure as a painter. she has her paintings covered up with blankets and towels, she is so ashamed. all her friends come to her house and peek under the covers and say things like, "wow," and "really fine." Brett thinks they are all liars.

Jacob, likewise, thinks he stinks as a writer. he hides his poems and short stories and songs in drawers. all his friends would peek in Jacob's drawers, but they don't even know he has fine works of art hidden there. they are unaware that Jacob is a drawer poet. once or twice a year, when Jacob gets very drunk or temporarily very secure, he takes a secluded poem out and reads it aloud. his friends say things like, "wow," and "really fine," and Jacob thinks they are all liars.

Brett and Jacob smile at their friends who have good intentions and know they are only being polite. nobody really likes their work, not even their parents who praise them long distance.

Being good to yourself is the hardest task there is. writing a novel (even winning the Nobel Prize) is nothing in comparison to LOVING YOURSELF.

For moments at a time, Brett and Jacob overcome their inferiority complexes. they think: i'm really a great artist with tons of potential. someday soon i will be famous. i'll be rich. i'll show them. all of them. when Brett and Jacob feel this way, they often do a cute little tap dance in front of the mirror and smile adoringly at their own adorable image. they sing about being beautiful people. they are all alone and no one is listening so they feel free to improvise. they try hard in the mirror to believe all the nice things they are singing to themselves. they wink and smile and pinch their own cheeks.

Brett: you paint such lovely pictures. and you have a gorgeous face and long, silky blonde hair! tra la.

Jacob: you are a great poet, kiddo. you have fabulous muscles and thick black curly hair. you sexy son-of-a-bitch, Jacob Moscovitz! da dum . . .

All this self-adoration lasts a moment or two before fading into the woodwork and fogging up the mirrors.

11 WALK AWAY FROM SOMETHING. where is there to go? that's a good question, but don't ask it. dance in the sunlight instead. if there is no sunlight, dance in a well-heated room, but don't ask trap questions. let sleeping dogs lie. let all animals lie. if it's cold outside, wear an extra sweater under a winter coat that is fully lined and walk away from something that doesn't warm you up. the hole you create leaves room for the breeze of something fresh and fertile to blow in and plant itself interestingly in your path.

Brett: maybe if we walk, Jacob, new answers will come to us?

Jacob: i don't feel like moving. my muscles are sore from working under the car.

Brett: they say oxygen is good for muscles as well as for making decisions.

Jacob (sardonically): yeah. so you take a walk for both of us and make nice, clear decisions in the fresh air. i'm going to stay in this stuffy apartment and make my own stale decisions in peace and quiet!

Brett: you're impossible!

Brett slams the door behind her and walks dramatically down the block, blowing steam into the cold air and swearing under her hot breath. suddenly, she spies her best friend, Annie, wearing a vanilla trench coat and hiking boots, on her way home from the library. a productive,

moving day propels Annie down the street, her vanilla energy gaily slapping against the cement below.

Brett: wow, Annie, am i glad to see you!

Annie: Brett, have you been crying?

Brett: just a little. that damned Jacob, he's . . .

Annie: impossible.

Brett: exactly.

Annie: well, when are you going to give it up, kid?

Brett: i don't know. it seems so futile, barren at times,
and then, spontaneously, it gets better

Annie: for three minutes?

Brett: no. usually longer. still, it is ruining my youth,
not to mention my god damn figure!

Annie: donuts again?

Brett: croissants. and tons of wine! it's the only way i
can relax around him.

Annie: men!

Brett: yeah . . . they're fattening.

Annie: hey. come over to my house? have some tea
without crumpets. get away from him for awhile. change
perspective. it's healthy. hey listen, i'm having a pot luck at
my house tonight. some really fine women from my depart-
ment. why not join us? what you need Brett, is new stimula-
tion.

Brett: i don't know Annie. sounds good but something
tells me i need to take a long walk alone for my circulation,
then go back and talk this thing out, once and for all! make
a decision about this relationship. i'll call you.

Annie: oh well, suit yourself. but it's too bad. you're
going to miss a terrific dinner. i'm making *coq au vin.*

Brett: damn, my favorite.

Annie: seems you have stronger appetites elsewhere?

Brett: o Annie . . .

Annie (touching Brett's shoulder affectionately): don't
worry about it. call me. either way's fine. there's always
plenty at these things.

Brett walks away from Annie, a genuine upper in her
life, towards Jacob, who verges on being a genuine downer.
why does Brett move in these strange ways? who knows.

15

early childhood training and years and years of practice are good, educated guesses.

Jacob is sitting, absolutely immobile in his dimly lit, poorly ventilated apartment, anxiously awaiting Brett's return so he can act annoyed that she came back so early.

Brett and Jacob continually create their own karma, even though they aren't aware of it. they could get along just fine if they developed more love karma to replace all their hate karma. it's quite simple, really, if you commit yourself to overcoming history.

Brett marches into Jacob's flat, having taken a long, brisk walk which did her circulation no good.

Brett: it takes two to tango, Jacob. if you stopped fighting with me, i wouldn't get bitchy.

Jacob: oh yeah? seems to me it's you who's always finding fault with me. i'm perfectly satisfied with things as they are.

Brett: you're perfectly satisfied to have no communication, work on your car, eat pizza and say we have a nice, healthy relationship when we have no relationship at all!

Jacob: there you go again.

Brett: you're so thick-headed.

Jacob: so go find someone else, if you're not happy.

Brett: i may just do that. don't push your luck. Annie invited me to a pot luck tonight. i just may go. i may go a lot of places, Jacob. there are plenty of fish in the sea, and don't count on me to stick around you much longer drowning in this crap of yours!

Jacob: hey come on. don't start. you're just getting yourself all upset. listen, i've got to go downtown to pick up a few parts. why don't i bring some ice cream back and we'll just relax tonight, take it easy, huh?

Jacob takes Brett in his arms and surrounds her with gentle kisses. he always acts adoringly when he suspects he might lose Brett, especially to women friends.

Brett (melting a bit): a double?

Jacob: shit, a half gallon if you stop fighting.

Brett: god damn it, Jacob.

Jacob: o.k., i'm sorry. it takes two to tango. you're right. trust me, honey. i'll be back soon. then we'll really dance.

Jacob almost lost his love to *coq au vin*. it was a close contest between chicken and butter pecan. is it dishes or men who win a woman's taste? is it possible to change one's deepest appetites?

12 NEWS BULLETIN: on the way home from the ice cream parlor, the ice cream melted. Jacob got so involved with car parts, he was an hour late. Brett cried. Jacob yelled. they broke up a few minutes later. neither of them got any ice cream or sex that particularly disjointed evening.

. . .

In spite of disappointments like the above, Brett is truly glad she entered her ill-fated relationship with Jacob. the experience has made her soul richer. suffering makes us earthy. Brett is equally glad she ended the affair after only three days. just when she began to smell disaster. what does disaster smell like? who knows. but Brett smelled it. most people don't. most people take an average of twenty years or even a whole lifetime to recognize the smell of a rotten relationship. most people have clogged up olfactory glands.

Most people are cowards when it comes to smelling loneliness and fear. not Brett. not quite. she is acquiring independence and strength. she's been in a women's group and her consciousness is getting pretty high. it's already miles above average, though miles below perfect. still, she doesn't let men fuck with her brain or body unless she absolutely wants them to. she is partially liberated. hunger is an awfully powerful state of mind. it can throw off all the senses, all five or six of them, including the sense of smell. Brett's senses are in a pretty good place, not a great place, but a pretty good one.

13 JACOB IS WORKING on his car.
Jacob is working on his car.
Jacob is working on his car.
etcetera.

14

I AM WORKING on these characters. i understand them in parts. i understand myself in parts. we all understand things in parts; it's a fragmented universe we walk around in.

If you don't believe this you're fooling yourself. you're one of those obnoxious characters in other people's novels who has it "all together"; none of my characters would be caught dead with it "all together." mellow yellow is impossible. it is a made-up figment of the imagination. people who claim to be mellow yellow are pretending. they are truly liars. i know a lot of them and they put on a good act with their teethy smiles and vacant gazes and their ability to flex their bodies into the shape of a pretzel, but when it comes down to brass tacks, they don't know what they're doing anymore than we do.

Some examples of mellow-yellow pretenders are EST graduates, Moonies, Macrobiotics, Scientologists, and Gestalt therapists. statistics show that these people suffer just as many stomach cramps, headaches (including severe migraines), as many visits to endocrinologists, psychoanalysts and podiatrists, have just as many fits of depression, as many pimples, fat thighs and nightmares as any random, American individual. they also eat an average amount of greasy pastry, and drink an average amount of cheap wine. they are nowhere near perfect, though they are perfectly normal. so don't feel nervous around them, and whatever you do, don't look to them for TRUTH, whatever that is. and don't give them your MONEY, if you happen to have any. beware of professional liars. they'll make you feel guilty for no reason at all.

My characters are more comforting. they have twitches and stutter and say silly things at the wrong time. my characters have pimples and cellulite and are trying harder to improve while admitting they make gross errors. they know they are no where near being mellow yellow. they are real types you can identify with.

Brett: i hope Jacob brings back a pint instead of a quart of ice cream. i've been eating too much lately. Annie is right. i've been feeding myself masochism lately instead

of proper nutrition. my thighs are suffering broad conse-
quences. who can i blame for all this self-destruction? my
mother? civilization? Baskin and Robbins? Jacob? my
senses? all of the above?

Jacob: i don't know about that Annie. she's a weirdo.
those sunglasses and trench coat are concealing something. why is she always with women? what does she have
against 50% of the population? she's trying to break up
Brett and i. i can sense it. i'll show her. i'll show 'em all. i'll
buy a quart of ice cream and a pint of hot fudge sauce. i'll
make Brett happy in spite of Annie. we'll fuck all night
long, and i'll stay erect for hours. i'll show those two. can
you imagine Brett choosing a lousy pot luck supper over a
night in bed with me? ha! actually, i've been worrying
about such things the last few days. in fact, lately, i've been
feeling unusually insecure. but Brett will never know. certainly Annie will never know. none of those witches will
find out! i'll keep it to myself, like i always do.

. . .

Yes, it's a fragmented world. nobody knows anyone
else completely. though god knows everyone tries.
examples are Brett and Jacob, Richard Burton and Elizabeth Taylor, China and the United States, and parents and
children.

The up-to-date precarious situation for our characters
is as follows: Jacob is incessantly under a 1963 Mercedes
Benz: a sociological fact sitting in his driveway. Brett is un-
endingly trying on clothes, applying make-up and freshen-
ing up. Elizabeth Arden products are expensive facts sitting
on the nightstand. Jacob is attempting to be daddy's little
mechanic, and Brett is trying to be daddy's little doll. Brett
and Jacob's lives are greatly complicated by accessories,
though they are barely aware of the great clutter. Brett's
clothes never quite fit. Jacob's car continually falls apart.
no one is fully satisfied. life continues in its frustrating and
fragmented fashion. like the characters, life doesn't always
run so well.

15 I HARDLY EVER TELL the truth, the whole truth and nothing but the truth and that is because i don't know what it is so help me whoever you are.

16 INTRODUCING BUDDY: a character sitting next to me in this cafe while i'm working on the novel. he's a professional. he's got a professional job, and a professional smile. why he's got professional TEETH and a fat professional checking account.

It's harder than you think, Buddy. i am telling this creep about my life, God knows why. being an artist isn't as romantic as it sometimes seems, especially to outsiders like you. i tell him i've got holes in my jeans and holes in my teeth and holes in my heart. i've got to create my own structure, day in and day out. i ain't got nobody to tell me what my job in life is. what my purpose is. what i got to do in order to be a MEANINGFUL PERSON. i don't have to be anywhere at any specific time.

Buddy: well, you must feel fortunate about that?

Author: you think it's a luxury, Buddy? well, it drives me crazy, sometimes.

Buddy: but you seem so carefree, so alive. i admire a girl with spirit.

Author: i bet you admire quarter horses too.

. . .

What does he know? being free is not easy. sometimes i have to walk it off. for miles and miles and miles, this is ARTISTIC FREEDOM. i tell this professional all about it and he just keeps telling me how lucky i am to avoid rush hour traffic on the Bay Bridge everyday. he just keeps displaying his professional pearly whites at me and patting me on the back.

He doesn't know shit, i think to myself, while smiling pleasantly and professionally back at him. i mean we are in a public place, after all. i can't spit at him in the middle of a groovy cafe?

Maybe my life would be simpler if i married a fat, rich boring slob like him? i think weird concoctions of thoughts and images to myself to keep my mind busy. yeah, then i'd really have something specific to bitch about, instead of just free-floating anxiety. you can't call up your friends on the telephone and complain daily about free-floating anxiety as easily as you can complain about a rotten, professional husband.

While i am tossing images around, Brett strolls by, her long, blonde hair swaying in the narrow aisles. Buddy turns his head 180 degrees in the direction of her ass. don't touch my character, i'm thinking, as i carefully watch his shifty eyes. don't you lay one of your sweaty, fat hands on her. fortunately for him (i am prepared to use self-defense techniques to protect and defend Brett's honor, not to mention body) he lets her pass without incident. he returns to our conversation only slightly visibly flustered.

Buddy: my, my. Brett certainly knows how to dress! that is such a smart suit she is wearing. i admire young girls who wear nice, smart clothes.

Author: how do you like my attire, Buddy? (i point to my levis and knit tee-shirt.)

Buddy: oh it's fine. the casual look is fine too. you're always clean and neat. that's important. but you must admit that Brett does have a particularly striking figure.

Author: of course i do. i created it! however, you might be interested in knowing, just for the record, that she took 47 minutes to get that particular "look" together this morning. it's no one-two-three job, Buddy. there's a lot of hard work behind the scenes . . . now, on the other hand, i got dressed in 3.4 minutes today.

Buddy: well, it doesn't show. you look rather nice to me. as if you spent at least 10 or 15 minutes preparing. your outfit is color-coordinated. that's more than i can say for a lot of young folks these days.

Author: thanks for the compliments, Buddy. but it doesn't matter to me. i'm not into style and physical image to the degree that Brett is. we had pretty different childhoods, she and i. my parents, thankfully, gave me support for my brain, at least part of it. so i didn't always have to be preoccupied with dressing to kill. if you know what i mean.

Buddy: of course i do. that was very nice of your parents. mine were a bit more like Brett's, i'm afraid. i mean they *were* quite clothes conscious.

    Author: is that why you're dressed to kill?

    Buddy (blushing): oh my. am i really?

            . . .

You know, actually, i wouldn't marry Buddy, even if he were the very last professional on earth. even if i was starving to death and he had the last bologna sandwich and was willing to share it. i don't say this out loud, of course. why be impolite in my most favorite hang-out?

I hold onto my friends instead. if they are not nearby, i hold them in my mind. i say things like: let's get naked and dance our crazy asses off. i say: let's fart in Buddy's face. i say these things to my brain and my brain alone, and it feels instantly better. i massage my thoughts with peculiar illusions that work better than any product on the market, including alka seltzer. the condition of my angry colon, for example, improves vastly after 3 or 4 such thoughts. all in all, dialogues with myself probably extend my life expectancy.

I also sing: get lost Buddy and other men who have money, professional teeth and ties and very little else songs. then i sing love songs to my friends. "thank god you exist" are a few of the lyrics. sometimes i sing all these tunes simultaneously; it's my own kind of harmony.

17 BRETT WANTS TO BE with Jacob. or some man, or some woman. just someone. a person. someone still breathing. deeply enough. just so it's love. so it's REAL. Jacob feels the same way, but he won't talk about it. he prefers tightening nuts and bolts. he prefers the perfection of machinery. the hum of a well-tuned car. it frightens him less than the hum of a well-tuned lover. that's all. it's a survival mechanism. everybody has one. right? of course they do. Jacob wants to be with Brett very, very badly, but instead of calling her on the telephone, he's adjusting his valves. it's perfectly normal.

On the way to the auto parts store, Jacob runs into Annie; for some unexplained reason, he braves a confrontation.

Jacob: why do you hate me, Annie?

Annie: i don't hate you. you just get in the way.

Jacob: but i'm trying harder.

Annie: can't you try harder somewhere else?

Jacob: you mean away from Brett?

Annie: why can't you work on yourself instead of screwing up women, driving them crazy with all your male consciousness-raising crap?

Jacob: what i need to work out involves being with a woman. i can't do it in a vacuum.

Annie: but i suppose you can do it under the car?

Jacob: very funny. Annie, do you know what you are? you're a MALE HATER. you're full of women's lib poison!

Annie: you're just plain full of it!

Jacob: you just want to break Brett and me up so you can have a crack at her, right?

Jacob laughs. continuously amused by his own unique brand of humor.

Annie: i won't even waste my breath answering that one. Jacob, you are a true pig, a pure breed. you are not only filthy on the outside but apparently all the way through. according to you, feminism is a lesbian plot, right, out to get you? all your girlfriends are going to be dragged away by wild amazons. have you ever heard of FRIEND-SHIP? probably not.

Jacob (flustered): i'm not responsible for your warped perceptions of men!

Annie: you *are* responsible for what you're doing to Brett, for all the ways you upset her. being in a lousy men's group—"admitting it" doesn't let you off the hook.

Jacob: Jesus, you're so intense about everything. you'd drive me crazy!

Annie (smiling slyly): well, don't worry. you're not going to get the chance.

Jacob: listen. can't we get along? Brett chooses to be with me, you know. it's not my fault. i can't help it if she happens to be in love with me!

Annie initiates the goodbyes. while they are march-ing off in opposite directions, Jacob is thinking: wow. it's a shame. she's a knockout. great eyes. and she's so quick . . . however, Jacob is committed to talking his brain into ego-elevating thoughts at all times. he's *not* into taking chances, especially with women. right now he is convincing his mind that Annie is a creepy, stupid slob. he is repeating a mantra over and over again until he brainwashes his brain. it makes life easier (bearable) for Jacob thinking he detests women he secretly is dying to sleep with. it is too painful and frightening to let his brain realize he admires a woman who is indifferent to him. engaging in self-controlled meditations puts Jacob back on top of things, where he thinks he belongs.

. . .

Everyone seems to be taking a walk today, because just a block after leaving Jacob, Annie runs into Brett. some days people make greater strides towards available oxygen than on other days. on their pilgrimage towards fresh air, Annie and Brett delightfully collide.

Brett: i'm sorry i didn't make it last night, Annie.

Annie: that's o.k. Brett. is everything all right?

Brett: yeah, well, sort of. how was the pot luck?

Annie: wonderful! you're just going to have to meet these women. you'll love them. we ate and drank and laughed for hours. it's so comfortable being with women . . . hey, kid. why not come to dinner tonight?

Brett: are you having *coq au vin?*

Annie: for god's sake. i don't have it every night. hey, are you just interested in my cooking? how about the company?

Brett: i was just kidding!

Annie (smiling): i know!

Brett: i really want to come over and soon! we've got to get together more often. it's just this crap . . . you know all this stuff with Jacob. it's taken all my time away. i've been realizing that lately.

Annie: i know. you're too busy fighting with him to have fun anymore with your friends?

Brett: oh Annie. that isn't so. i'm not going to forget my friends.

Annie: seriously, Brett. i've been there. and i understand. i want you to know that i'm here for you whenever
you need to talk. whenever you need me. . . i know it's not
an easy time for you. just remember that when the going
gets rough.

Brett: gets rough! is rough. most of the time.

Annie: yeah. well, are you going to come to dinner? it's
macaroni and cheese so if you come i know it's out of love,
right?

Brett: you're great, Annie. you always make me laugh.
it's so good for my spirit.

Annie: and mine!

Brett: listen, pal. i really would come tonight, but the
author already invited me to dinner, and she's pretty sensitive you know. under a lot of stress writing this book.

Annie: is Jacob coming too?

Brett: are you kidding? hell no! it's just me and Susan
tonight. we need to talk. spend some quiet time together.

Annie: sounds great. well, any day this week would be
fine. i'll be home most evenings working, so come when it
feels right for you. just call me by five or so.

Brett: it's a deal. before the week is out we'll dine together. let's hug on it. (they embrace, then break apart.)
from now on let's do it once a week like in the good old
days, huh?

Annie: fine with me. i'd love it. love *you!*

Brett: God, me too, Annie. you're so important to me.
whenever i see you i realize: *i miss you.* (they embrace
again, a little longer and a little wider.)

Brett thinks to herself: Annie's hugs always feel so
warm and full. but thank god at least tonight i'll avoid all
those damn carbohydrates in her macaroni and cheese.

18 I'VE INVITED Brett and Jacob to Chapter Eight-
een. no, Brett doesn't know about Jacob; she
wasn't lying. i do have good intentions, though. i'm hoping
for a reconciliation between them. i think they really want
one. don't laugh. everything is possible and worth pursuing.
some people get married two or three times before they

really decide. it's typical. Brett and Jacob really are quite typical. most people are. never knowing exactly how you feel is quite typical, indeed.

Brett: i'm working on getting in touch with my feelings.

Jacob: i'm working on my manifold.

Brett: i think i'm finally getting in touch with who i really am.

Jacob: i finally got the last nut off. it was rusted.

Brett: i think i'm ready for a deep, meaningful relationship.

Jacob: i feel filthy. i'm ready for a shower.

These are just a few typical thoughts Brett and Jacob and everyone else have all the time.

. . .

Neither of my characters knows the other is coming to this fabulous dinner party. i'm deceiving them for their own sake. playing tricks in order to make them deliciously happy. i'm a romantic idealist as well as an international cook. i can't help it. it's my chemistry. what's a few white lies, and sauces anyway, in the name of pure and simple love and gourmet FOOD?

They're not here yet . . . tick tick tick. i think they are playing hard to get. maybe they'll show up in Chapter Nineteen? who knows. tick tick tick. those selfish ingrates! they have their nerve being an hour late to an eight course soup to nuts feast. oh well, in case they don't show, i'm not going to get indigestion over it. i have an alternative plan. i'm going to tell you about writing in the basement!

. . .

I didn't know when i invented Brett and Jacob that they would turn out to be so errant, erratic and late for supper. so much for the great American couple, who are, in fact, just two average American neurotics: over-sensitive and under-aware.

Brett: i'm staying home to work on my poetry. home's the only safe place for me lately. it's where my heart lies most easily. i feel torn, actually shredded, is more like it, by everyone who comes near me.

Jacob: i think i'll hide out in the basement tonight, and gain control of the situation. just because the author invites me to dinner, doesn't mean i have to go.

Author: well, they didn't show up or, in other words, 11:30 is pretty late to expect anyone to arrive for an eight course meal; it's even getting late for a snack. so tick tick, as promised (*i* keep my promises) i'm going to tell you everything you always wanted to know about writing in the basement and were afraid to ask. writing in the basement is pretty heavy. especially in the middle of the night. like three in the morning. it's even heavier if you have a cat which sits on your lap while you're writing and plays with your face and the typewriter keys. it's much too cold and dark in the basement. writing at three in the morning is dark enough! so i stay away from subterranean writing.

Someday i may write in the basement again. someday i may write with a cat on my lap. who knows? everything is in flux, even basements and cats. everything is possible, even love. WALKING VANILLA is possible. even in the basement. even cats could most likely walk with vanilla. yes, the future holds a lot of possibility in storage for us all.

Jacob: you can write in the basement. buy a space heater. create your own desired temperature. avoid the chill. the author should have taken a home maintenance course. there are endless possibilities in the basement. i could build you what you need.

Brett: no you couldn't. it's not in your hands.

Jacob: i have power tools.

Annie: but no power.

19 PEOPLE ACT CRAZY. mothers for example, sit on bus stops yelling at children and slapping their faces. why? for no particular reason except that it's something they've learned to do instead of thinking about how unhappy and angry they are. that's how crazy some people get. and fathers come home and ignore their children. ignore their wives. ignore everybody and everything. they yell at their wives for spending money, even on toilet

paper. even on ground round beef for dinner! people are that bananas.

of course, you won't find these extreme kinds lurking between the covers of this novel. i leave these types on bus stops or in downtown offices. i walk right by them. no weirdos in baggy gray pants exposing himself in the bushes of this book. Brett and Jacob might not do you any good but they certainly won't do you harm. they won't slap your face, expose themselves or rile your children with their personal violence. (t.v. will do that.)

Brett: my father used to hit me with a thick black belt.

Jacob (clowning): was dad a karate expert?

Brett: why can't you be serious about anything, Jacob? i'm trying to share my life with you!

Jacob: why is everybody getting so heavy today? can't we be light for the holidays. Christ. i thought *you* wanted to get along. is this how you co-exist, Brett, picking at every word i say? screaming all the time and discussing past tortures? let's have a beer. a few laughs. a kiss?

Brett: do you love me, Jacob? i mean do you feel me inside you?

Jacob: of course i do, what are you CRAZY? boy, am i going to show you how much. you gorgeous creature, you! i'm going to show you what love is!

they tumble and roll. they roll and tumble on the thick red rug. Jacob has trouble distinguishing between love and sex. actually, he's afraid to recognize the great difference, so he pretends they are exactly the same thing.

20 YES, WE CAN SEE that Brett and Jacob have their problems, their typical everyday problems. the main one being that they wish they were someone else 85% of the time; 72% of the time they wish they had somebody else's body; 67% of the time they wish they had someone else's personality; and 97% of the time, they wish they had someone else's checking account.

Brett: Christmas is so depressing, Jake. i can't afford to buy anybody anything.

Jacob: it's the thought that counts.

Brett: well, that's what i'm going to give everybody. a bunch of my thoughts.

Jacob: good ones, i hope?

Like most people, Brett and Jacob want to be thin, thinner, most thin. and like most people, they are never satisfied. for instance, 54% of the human race with straight hair wish they had curly locks, and vice versa. 63% of married people wish they were divorced and 64% of divorced people wish they were married. similar statistics exist for short and tall people, young and old, employed and unemployed citizens. all data point to the notion that the grass is greener in somebody else's life. the sad facts support our theory that most people will never get what they want.

Those of us who find a few things in life that really taste good are very lucky. remember that. you are among the most fortunate human tasters on the face of the globe. APPRECIATE YOUR TONGUE. it gives you more moments of pure pleasure than you give it credit for.

Author: Brett and Jacob went to sleep and left me alone here with a half liter of wine and Tuna Melitta, the cat. Annie is here too, doing research. i'm pretending she's not here in order to make this scene appear most dramatic: THE NOVELIST ALL ALONE IN THE BASEMENT WITH VIN ROSE, WRITING UNTIL THE SUN COMES UP.

. . .

Brett and Jacob are not sleeping. the author, contrary to popular belief, doesn't know everything. Brett and Jacob took a brief nap, but are up and at it again. at what? at spying on the author in the middle of the dramatic night, that's what.

Jacob: see. she's with Annie again. why are they together so much?

Brett: Jacob, you have one thing on your mind. they are good friends. they are both writers. they both tend to stay up late working. as you can see, they are both hard at work right now. it's nice to have company. sometimes, you ask the dumbest questions, Jacob.

Jacob: that Annie is a troublemaker.

29

Brett: she is not. she's a good friend of mine, and i would appreciate it if you would stop taking your hostility out on her. she doesn't criticize me like you do. *she* lets me be, and i happen to appreciate that! she's a healer, not a troublemaker. you're that.

Jacob: thanks, dear. i'm real happy for you and your great friendships! maybe if you acted half as nice to me as you do to them, we'd get along. Annie is always picking on me. it's not my fault.

Brett: you ask for it. why don't you try to get along?

Jacob: because she hates men.

Brett: that's not true.

Jacob: she sure acts like it. why can't she be more like the author, who at least is pleasant to me and tries to understand me a little. wow. the author is a gem compared to that rock of Gibraltar. you'd think by spending so much time around the author, some generosity and kindness would rub off on Annie.

Brett: Jacob, you know what's bugging you. you're pissed off because Annie doesn't make a big fuss over you. you expect every woman to adore you.

Jacob: that's not true. why would i want her to be attracted to me? it would only be a pain since i'm not the slightest bit interested. look at her. she's always got her damn nose in a book. zero sex appeal.

Brett: hey, look. i think they heard us. they're coming to the window. let's split.

Jacob: yeah! the last thing i want is for Annie to catch me spying on her. she might get the wrong idea. can you imagine that?

Brett: i can imagine anything when it comes to you and sex, Jacob. your sexual fantasies are unreal!

Jacob: oh yeah. well, let's go back to bed and make them real.

21 I DON'T SMOKE ANYMORE. Brett smokes. so does Jacob. in fact, they are both chain-smokers, moderate drinkers, and heavy sugar freaks. they are artists, so they do these perverse things. i'm an artist too, so i've had to exercise great restraint to avoid the inclination to stick a Winston in my mouth. now that i don't inhale nicotine, i chew things. crackers/toothpicks/carrots/pencils/fingernails. anything i can get my teeth on. i'm a junkie. i admit it. we all have a similar dilemma to face:

WHAT TO DO WITH THE LEFTOVER ENERGY AFTER THE CIGARETTES HAVE GONE AWAY?

It's another good question. maybe writing this novel is the answer. maybe, maybe not.

22 AFTER A BUBBLE BATH, Brett is sitting at her typewriter in a long, white terrycloth robe, wanting desperately to write a tragic poem about her tragic relationship with Jacob Moscovitz, and be done with it! she wants thereby to make her work more weighty and intense than the relationship itself. it's one approach to backing out of the rut she's found herself in. one way to dilute the muddy waters of love. Brett stares languidly at the pot of French roast coffee freshly brewed in the melitta pot; she puffs a Winston ciagrette. she draws a blank.

23 JACOB IS WORKING on his car. his hands are greasy. he rubs his eyes with his greasy hands. now his eyes are greasy. nothing else to report as yet.

24 Author: the way Jacob works on his car is not living in the moment, not anymore.

Buddy: how do you know that? he seems quite involved.

Author: Jacob has a cluttered brain. having a cluttered brain that races ideas around the brain track is the opposite of living in the moment. Jacob has grown twisted, complicated and clogged with ideas, so he is in trouble with the clock. he hears it ticking too much. this trouble is typical. it begins around the age of eleven. this is due to the onset of puberty. sex takes us out of the moment and into the WOODS.

It has done that to Brett and Jacob. they are perfect examples of being in the metaphoric woods. Brett is sitting at her desk staring into space, looking back on a crummy, three day romance she hardly cares about or remembers. she is trying to concoct a silly, tragic feeling out of a vague memory in order to write a silly tragic poem which has a lot of universal clarity. it's a bunch of wasted energy. an exhausting hike that goes nowhere.

Buddy: is Brett's poem going to be about being in the woods?

Author: hopefully it will be about getting out.

Buddy: now Jacob, he's completely different. he's accomplishing something!

Author: yes, Jacob is certainly different. he's working twelve hours a day on his car. he is obsessed with pistons and rings and valves. why? in order to avoid thinking about his feelings, in order to avoid the MOMENT. in their very different and unique ways, Brett and Jacob are both spaced-out of the moment, trapped in the thickly tangled woods of their brains, without any access to what is really going on in the wide-open spaces of their hearts.

25 I HAVE NEVER LOVED ANYONE AS MUCH AS I WOULD LIKE TO.

. . .

NOBODY HAS EVER LOVED ME AS MUCH AS I WOULD LIKE THEM TO.

26 MY CHARACTERS FEEL pretty much as i do. how do you feel? don't be afraid to admit it if you feel DEPRIVED. especially during the holidays. deprivation typically creeps into people's bones by late December. but let's not let deprivation get us completely down. let's put our hiking boots on and tie our winter laces and slide into vanilla hearts. into snow. into clear. into the best parts of the holiday spirit. into melting. into love. into song. and leave all our troubles behind!

Buddy: i don't have any hiking boots.

Author: that's just as well, Buddy.

27 BRETT IS STILL SITTING upright at her typewriter. she has written two lines (she doesn't particularly like them) of her new poem in 54 minutes. she has gone through a pack of Winston cigarettes and a full pot of French roast coffee in two hours and ten minutes. she is wired. she is angry. she is conscious of time/all of it. past/ present and future. she is conscious of tenses/all of them. present-perfect/imperfect/impossible. she's having trouble with the clock *and* the English language. when the phone rings, she thinks: whoever that is is a son-of-a-bitch. at her wits' end, she uncontrollably yells into the receiver.

Brett: yeah, who is it?

Jacob: Brett. it's me. please don't hang up. what are you yelling about?

Brett: i wasn't going to hang up. my God. what's the matter with you, Jacob? lately, you're so jumpy.

Jacob: well, God, the way you answered the phone! sounded like you were ready to kill.

Brett (brusquely): o.k., Jacob. what do you want?

What does Jacob want? who knows. he wants to talk. about what? about everything apparently.

Jacob: i want to talk about the way we left each other on Friday.

Brett: Thursday.

Jacob: o.k., o.k. Thursday. whatever. what difference does it make? we need to talk about it.

Brett: i'm busy working, Jacob.

Jacob: painting?

Brett: no. actually i happen to be writing a poem about this ridiculous relationship of ours.

Jacob: see! that's what we need to talk about. the way we constantly cut each other. give me an hour, Brett. that's all i ask. then if you want to write a whole book of poems about hating me i promise not to bother you at all.

Brett you're really something, Jacob. you *really are!* i never said anything about hating you or what the poem was about.

Jacob: well, the way you answered the phone. not

seeing each other. you know, things get out of proportion, when we don't see each other.

Brett: they get more out of proportion when we do. speaking of constantly cutting into each other, that is precisely what you're doing with my time right now. don't you have any respect for my time alone. for my work?

Jacob: of course i do, honey. come on. i'm not asking for a whole day or something. just an hour. give me a chance?

Jacob really wants to make a connection. he wants to talk about sex. about communication. about his car. about fighting. about art/life/men/women and all the various combinations thereof. about feelings. the deepest ones. it's a rare moment for Jacob. if Brett is smart she'll take advantage of this talkative time in Jacob's life. who knows? it may be a once in a lifetime event.

Brett: i don't know, Jacob. i don't want to lose the mood of this poem by going out of the house.

Brett has definitely decided one thing: she is not going to do today what she has done in the past. she is not going to invite Jacob into her house/her space/her bed. her herstory is different in that respect in the present. she is still going to invite him into her time. but only a small portion of it.

Jacob: well, i could come over there?

Brett: no. i'm sorry, Jacob. that won't work today.

Jacob. o.k. then, neutral territory. meet me at the Mediterraneum. we can have a cup of coffee and clear things up.

Brett has an urge to hang up on Jacob and return to her tragic poem, her creative process, her own form of getting grounded. she is thinking: love is something that interrupts creative work. even "not love" interrupts it. while she is contemplating these serious thoughts, she answers Jacob.

Brett: all right. but i only have half an hour. it's really a very busy day for me.

Brett agrees to meet with Jacob only to get rid of him. people get together under the pretense of reconciliation, only to have the opportunity to shout. to punch somebody in the nose or raise their blood pressure with a rip-roaring argument. yes. a lot of people like to wake up their bloodstream with a good wrestling match. even a bloody nose or a black eye turns some people on. really! there are types that actually adore the crude ornaments achieved in combat. yes, it is often true that when someone says, "you were just asking for that," THEY WERE. it happens on every street, on every corner, in every alley of the great big ring called life. a lot of people (not just boxers!) thrive on dissonance, bruises, and the attention of horrified crowds.

. . .

Jacob: i'll show Brett! i'll show Annie. i'll show the women's movement. i'll show everybody in the damn neighborhood, even if the punks aren't watching. i'm going to fight this thing to the finish line. (Jacob does a little sparring with himself in the mirror, before taking off for the battlefield.)

Brett and Jacob both know they will break up again and again. they both know they will get badly bruised in the process. but, it's a habit with them. they can't help it. they can't break up with disaster. maybe they really don't want to. maybe it's too physiologically stimulating. maybe it's a giant thrill to their nervous systems. being upset and bouncing around in agitated conditions.

Hanging up the telephone, Brett goes directly to the bathroom mirror, though she had intended on returning to her typewriter, which is in the dining room. she had every intention of finishing her poem before preparing to go outdoors. odd, isn't it, how even smart cookies like Brett don't know which room they're going to next. so, how are we supposed to figure them out or find them for god's sake? we can't. we cannot predict people's detailed movements (even dancers) but we can take notes and make movies while they are in motion.

Brett goes into the bathroom and applies brown mascara and green eyeshadow, a moderate amount to her upper eyelids. she sprays ice blue secret deodorant generously to her underarms. she combs her long, blonde hair briskly with a 100% boar bristle brush, and brushes her

pearly white teeth with mint flavored Crest. see how carefully we are observing! Brett never wears lipstick or bras,
girdles or vaginal sprays. she looks good, not great, but
pretty good, considering the stress she's under. of course.
she usually does look tops since she is a tall attractive
blonde with good bone structure.

. . .

Jacob is waiting at a cafe table when Brett arrives. he
looks great. he has showered all the grease off his eyes and
hands. he is quite impressive. the contrast is immense. for
the first time in weeks, Jacob is greaseless. he has that
healthy look people get after working very hard for a long
time and then suddenly, they take a shower and put on a
turtleneck sweater and corduroy pants, instead of overalls.
it's the rugged look. Jacob looks especially rugged today.
he has worked at it. twenty-five minutes in the shower. one
hour total in the bathroom, shaving, trimming and applying
Brut cologne, and of course, posing in the mirror from the
most compelling and attractive angles imaginable. now,
selecting that most perfect view, and winning smile, Jacob
stares at Brett over the edge of his recently dry-cleaned
thick, black sweater; it's a pretty dramatic shot.

Jacob: hi, Brett.

Brett: hi, Jacob.

I have her say "hi" back very tentatively. she is not
going to lead this dialogue, even if Jacob leads it astray.
i've decided that much for sure; enough is enough. women
have talked for themselves and men long enough. it's
about time Jacob offered some revelations, even tiny ones.
he's going to initiate conversation, even if it is as a novice.
how else to gain experience than by starting out with a few
good words. Jacob is going to give us insights into his highly
concealed character by opening his mouth, even if he
stutters.

As a matter of fact, i am going to give Jacob the rest
of this chapter to spill the beans. to lay his soul on the
table. so everyone can at last see a man in touch with his
feelings/heart/woman. it would be good for men if they
talked about their feelings more often. maybe if they did

they could become friends with each other. or at least with themselves. maybe they could get some clues about what they are doing. so, here's your opportunity, Jacob, to unravel the mysteries of your inner self. don't say i never gave you the chance to discover the real you.

Jacob: it was pretty heavy on Friday (pause). i mean Thursday (pause). i think we were pretty rash, Brett (pause). i mean i was. (double pause) i've been thinking (pause). maybe we should give it another (pause) try. i mean i'm sorry for (pause) being so critical (triple pause). aren't you going to say anything?

Author (aside): no she isn't, you jerk.

Jacob: o.k., play hard to get. fine, swell. just 'cause i didn't like one painting. didn't make a big deal over it. you know i think you're a terrific painter. you know i'm honest with you. i'd say so if i didn't like your work. but i tell you it's great all the damn time. then you go crazy when i criticize one piece, one detail of one piece. you're too sensitive. it's you who doesn't believe in your work, not me (pause). you want me to be honest, don't you, Brett?

Jacob takes Brett's hand and holds it awkwardly. he is attempting to be gentle. it makes him sweat. his hand is dripping all over Brett's hand, which isn't entirely dry either.

Jacob: Brett, listen to me. i've missed you. i mean i really need you. i want to get along. i don't want to give up just like that.

He snaps his fingers, to break things up a bit. it is very, very hard for Jacob to hear himself say these words. they sound like they are coming from outerspace. from a martian, not from his own quivering lips. there is a tear in Jacob's left eye, which also appears odd and far away to Jacob himself. unusual physiological responses keep popping up in Jacob like unexpected varicose veins; it's like he is inhabiting somebody else's body. Jacob squeezes Brett's hand firmly; he needs to get a grasp on something. he is suddenly overloaded with emotions. he feels like he is floating instead of grounding. it frightens him. he hears a stranger's voice inside say over and over again. i'm scared.

i'm scared. i'm terrified of flying out too far. i'm afraid i won't come back to my center.

Jacob: hey Brett. lighten up, huh? (Jacob is thinking about how L.S.D. was nothing compared to the shifts in perception he is presently experiencing.)

Jacob means well, even when he's freaked out like this. most people do. but he doesn't know how to be honest. most people don't. Brett doesn't either. listen, here's evidence. i've got it all written down.

Buddy: so do i. this cafe scene is good drama. romantic setting. the fear of going crazy. reminds me of Fitzgerald. the lighting could be better but it will do. we can always add houselights and houseplants later for color if this gets produced.

Brett: i will not LIGHTEN UP. lay off me, Jacob!

Brett emerges from her trance. she comes out fighting like a champ, removing her sweaty hand from Jacob's sweaty hand. she realizes it's time for her to speak. it's tremendously admirable that she has waited this long, especially considering all the pauses/drama/and fear/of silence. both she and Jacob are dripping wet with emotion, at least at the hand stage.

Brett: hey, *you* lighten up! you don't know what you're talking about. it's *not* that you criticize my paintings that aggravates me. i couldn't care less. how come you never understand me? your god damn attitude drives me crazy!

Tears run down both of her eyes. women are twice as emotional as men, at least at the eye level/at water level. tears flow out of the female more readily. everyone knows that it's true but it's never been fully explained by experts. men and women both have tear ducts so originally it seems they were intended to cry an equal amount.

Brett: i like criticism! from my friends. it helps me to grow as an artist. as a person. in fact, i CRAVE IT. it's that arrogant way you lay things on me. the unfeeling aloofness, then all the paternalistic bullshit apologies and attempts to comfort me after it's *you* who's upset me to begin with. Jesus. you set the whole machinery going. it's a set up. it's maddening... and to top things off, of course, it all started after we got together that lovely romantic afternoon. big deal. so we had good SEX. everything has to change. before we slept together, you treated me like a person. can you remember that far back? when we were becoming friends? you men are all alike. don't deny it. i'm not going to listen. why don't you just go away and leave me alone so i can get something done! who needs this? who needs a bunch of crummy arguments with an idiot? not me!

Jacob: you're not yourself. calm down. all these feminists are doing wild things to your head.

Brett: THANK GOD.

Tears of sadness, and tears of rage run together very fast down her cheeks and all over Brett's Indian shirt. Jacob is stunned. he's mainly full of pauses now and internal combustion. both of them have twisted facial expressions. the scene isn't very pleasant nor is the couple very attractive anymore. even Jacob doesn't look particularly rugged at the moment, and Brett's bone structure is soggy.

They both have shaky hands, trembling thoughts. they both light cigarettes, and stare at different corners of the same cafe. they sense how very close they are, and how very far away. they hate each other intensely and lust after each other's bodies with equal and opposite vigor. they want to walk out and they want to walk into each other's arms. it's perfectly normal. it is simply the dialectical age they both live in.

Brett: i don't know why i waste my time/tears/words/breath.

She inhales deeply and blows a stream of thick smoke towards the corner of the cafe she is facing. in fact, she is actually talking to the corner by now. she is not looking at Jacob anymore. it's too painful. anger builds in Brett's colon and spills over into the rest of her body. especially her cheeks which are fire engine red. color enters Brett's face like a temperature. like a revolution. like an emergency blaze she doesn't want to put out.

Brett jumps up from the cafe table and walks out haughtily, smoking and bumping into chairs, tables and

strangers. she is trying to look perfectly cool, while simultaneously looking perfectly ridiculous.

. . .

Jacob sits perfectly still. perfectly alone. he shakes inside. he takes a long drag on his Lucky Strike which isn't
bringing him luck, and blows the smoke methodically into
the northwest corner of the cafe. his corner to concentrate
on today. people concentrate on the most curious objects
when they are avoiding each other. Jacob focuses intensely
on an empty cafe latte glass across the room; then he con-
templates a half empty glass of orange juice, wondering
why somebody didn't drink it all. the games he is playing
with his mind help him not to cry or shake externally or feel
anything dangerous. funny games distract him from going
nuts.

There are many communication tools we never
acquire while growing up, and where we grow up is not the
point. in Miami or Siberia, in the hottest sun or the coldest
wind, we still can't hear each other screaming for help.

Jacob: i get scared. sure i do. i admit it. but she'd never
know it. even if i shared it all, she'd ignore it. she really
doesn't want to know my feelings. once i shared my pain,
the whole bit with a woman i thought i could open up to.
she asked me to! and what did she do? she walked out on
me. i cried and fell on my knees and told her how lonely
and out of touch i felt. she got sick. she GOT SICK TO HER
STOMACH. i saw it. she thought i was a god damn whimp.
i'm not supposed to cry or get emotional in public, even in
private, and then i'm accused of being an insensitive
macho creep. i can't win. civilization is against me. i'm supposed to stay in control and work steadily on my car. it's
not easy knowing all this. what people expect of me is quite
a strain. all the while i am deteriorating. without a woman
who accepts me, i will disintegrate entirely. GOD DAMN
YOU, DAD! YOU MADE ME THE MACHINE I AM TODAY.
shit. i could have been a man. i could have been a person,
if you'd let me.

Jacob sighs in utter despair and exhaustion. he looks

around the cafe to see if he knows anyone. then he buries his heavy, pounding head in his arms and rests.

. . .

Brett: Annie is right. they're all alike at the critical cut-off point. but my early childhood training makes me stick to them like glue year after year. what a bird-brain i am. when will i be free of Prince Charming fantasies? or when will i at least meet a reasonable facsimile that allows me to do my work? i could settle for that. i don't expect much. i don't expect perfection. just something approximating HUMAN.

. . .

Jacob: how can she just leave me sitting here? maybe i'll pick somebody up, and get this grief out of my system. maybe that red-head over there. she isn't bad and i'm sure i saw her smile at me awhile ago. sure. that's going to get little princess independence where she lives!

Who am i kidding? why is everyone walking away from me? i'm shaking more and more every day. maybe i'm really falling apart. at twenty-eight? in my prime? with all my hard work and exercise? with my men's group for support? maybe i drink too much? maybe i should quit smoking. shit. maybe i should just drink more. i feel terrible. nobody cares. not even me.

I'll just keep busy. start playing basketball again. and tennis. sure that will help. (he's unconvinced.) i wish i didn't worry about my damn ego every second of every day. i wish i really loved Brett/anybody/just myself.

The lights go out in Jacob's brain temporarily and in his own arms, he sleeps.

. . .

Brett (more thoughts while walking farther away from the cafe): maybe i should go back. maybe i'm too hard on him. it's just that i can't let myself be taken advantage of anymore. letting go is so hard. inside i'm soft, vulnerable but he's not going to know it. inside i'm putty. i want to love so badly. to let my armor down at the right times. i wish we both weren't so corrupted and overprotected and stupid. i wish i didn't have fat thighs. i wish i could finish that crummy poem. finish something. anything. even this relationship. i wish things were different than they always are. i wish i were a lot nicer.

Both Brett and Jacob wish they were nicer. they *are,* in fact. it's just that their mean streaks are showing more lately than their beautiful streaks which are partly hidden by circumstance. it's just a matter of getting the inside stuff more outside. it's not as simple as it sounds. there is a lot of brain wave material to get through to make contact to the outside.

28 CONTACT IS HEALTHY. flesh can't hurt you. Brett and Jacob act like it does, sometimes. they hide out in their apartments for the expressed purpose of not touching. they think touching is dangerous. they don't realize that hiding out is much more dangerous. sharp blades are dangerous. dull thoughts like suicide are dangerous. touching is not.

. . .

Part of me is always OUTSIDE MYSELF watching the rest of me play funny tricks. it's like the movies for free. you can watch yourself all day and all night for free. you can show reruns and instant replays if you feel like it. schizophrenia has a bad reputation in our culture. but it's really not so bad. it's an underrated form of entertainment. it depends on what kind of movies you prefer, and besides, it can be a very economical form of therapy. self-help and home movies. never underestimate the value of talking to yourself. of being schizophrenic with an enthusiastic commitment. you'll save hundreds of dollars normally siphoned off by shrinks.

29 FRIENDS ARE THE MOST precious thing an artist has. hold onto your friends. hold on tight. it's a good investment. walk with vanilla with fulltime friends. it's fulfilling. especially if you are crazy and most groups and respected institutions kick you out, year after year after year. Brett and Jacob have a great deal to learn.

they are artists. they are crazy. they get kicked out of groups and institutions year after year, and still, they don't invest enough in friendship. they don't know how. they are frightened.

Set an example for them. help them by helping yourself. tell your friends your closet problems. it will lead you down the road to intimacy. it's a remarkable vanilla road. flow into your friends. melt into them. lift something from your chest/a burden/a ton of bricks/whatever is resting uncomfortably there. share your pain. share everything you can with fulltime friends. share your houseplants. share your oxygen. you can trust your fulltime friends to share back, usually.

Call a chum on the phone. make a date for coffee. splurge. buy flowered underwear. buy a gold choker. tell your friends all the nice things you think but never say. all those closet compliments. you only live once. probably. let the good vibes come through. tell yourself today is the first day of the rest of your life. tell yourself what a great time you are having. being a fulltime friend and getting OUTSIDE. hey, it's good to be alive in CHAPTER TWENTY-NINE!!

30 SOMETIMES, I THINK Brett and Jacob are writing this novel and are using me to bring them together in the same book. maybe they hold the strings? i wouldn't put it past them. i don't mind actually! being a vehicle for their lives. it keeps me running. right now i am running across town to the library. Brett has tracked down Annie, and i'm parking the car, while they have a little chat.

Brett: i hate to bother you while you're studying, Annie. but i just had to talk to somebody. boy do i need a reality check.

Annie: no problem. i need a break anyway. let's go outside, and get some air while we talk.

They walk out to the front steps of the public library. they sit on the grey cement wall surrounded by bright yellow daisies. it is a clean, refreshing scene, except for Brett's face which is smeared with mascara and swollen with tears. she's a mess again. Annie isn't surprised.

Annie: did Jacob call?

Brett: yes (hiccup).

Annie: and you met him?

Brett (hiccup): yes. but i was soooo calm at first. i was only going to listen a little and then say goodbye. i was sure i was safe. but somehow, we both started yelling and i walked out all upset. i almost broke my neck tripping over some dumb chair. maybe i shouldn't have walked out. oh, i don't know. i'm so confused lately. everytime i leave, i want to go back. and when i'm with him, i just want to get away from the whole damn mess. what am i going to do, Annie?

Brett falls into Annie's waiting arms. Annie quietly soothes the distraught lover by stroking her disheveled hair.

Annie: yes, i know. it's o.k. you're doing fine. you are beginning to see what isn't working for you. that's all. it's a PROCESS, Brett. you can't expect to change overnight. you're being too hard on yourself.

Brett (perking up): you mean you don't think i'm completely out of my mind? just awful and weak, Annie?

Annie: of course not!

Brett: i thought you'd...oh i don't know...you're always so understanding. i'm not used to that. i guess it's me who really thinks i'm a fool, not you.

Annie (smiling): well, i do think you act a little foolishly about certain unmentionables, but i never think you are a FOOL. my God, you're my dear friend. i love you.

Brett (beaming): and i love you!

Annie: my advice is: try to stay away from him, just for a few days anyway. get into yourself. what makes you feel good. it will clear your head up and then you'll be better prepared to decide what it is you do or do not want regarding Jacob...so, you're coming to dinner tonight, right?

44

Brett (sitting up on her own power): wouldn't miss it. macaroni and cheese?

Annie: no. *coq au vin*. o.k.?

Brett: really? you're kidding!

Annie: well, leftovers.

Brett: i'll bring some wine.

Annie: great. listen. are you all right?

Brett: yeah. much better, naturally, after talking to my favorite physician.

Annie: well, in that case, favorite patient, take some further advice. do something especially nice for yourself this afternoon.

Brett: right on. i'm going to the Y and take a sauna. get rid of some of these toxins floating in my blood. i'll see ya tonight. i can't wait. thanks Annie.

. . .

Brett and Jacob are full of toxins, which cause their brains to be in a constant state of confusion. here are some of their latest confused thoughts:

Jacob: i want to overpower Brett. i just played a damn good game of tennis. i've got to get out on the court more often. i want to open up more in my men's group. i want Brett and i to talk, to be pals, to really listen to each other. i wonder why all my tennis and basketball and weight lifting doesn't help my skinny arms develop? i never want to see her again. she destroys my vision/my self-image. she makes me nervous. she has fat thighs. why should i be nervous. and cellulite. she's nowhere near perfect herself. i have a twitch in my left eye. i'd rather work on my car than fight with her. it's easier on my body than love. i don't have any real friends. and i don't know how to make them. i'm losing my grip.

Brett: he's so thick-headed. who's any better? he doesn't know his emotions from his carburetor. it's winter, and i do love lying in his warm arms, even if they are skinny. i want to be soft with someone. not just anyone. if we had a solid relationship, i might be able to quit smoking. where are my cigarettes? having one's work is not enough. it's so peaceful for awhile, but then i get hungry for more. my sinuses are clogged up. i want to be alone. i want a margarita. i'll take a sauna before i decide what to do with my life.

. . .

Down deep inside both these characters is the conviction that they will be happier if they are in love. even if they are pretending. they are children of the media/of the movies/of the television and the GREAT AMERICAN DREAM. they believe everything they see and hear. they are deaf, dumb and blind to the facts, which are: love is rare, tragic and brief. someone dies or leaves for Europe. or finds another, better lover. it's typical but challenging. everyone keeps moving, changing partners, getting evicted from romance, looking around for something special, and everyone is perpetually hungry for love. everyone wants it and hardly anybody has it. where is it?
HEY, LOVE. WHERE ARE YOU? ARE YOU HIDING OUT?

. . .

Instead of love, some people buy condominiums, cocktail dresses, expensive champagne, gooseliver pate and baguettes. some people buy time/egg nog/binoculars and Johnny Walker scotch. people buy all sorts of gizmos made out of plastic, and in Berkeley, they buy things made out of wood and wool and wax. the cash register rings all over the world. ring. ring. ring. can't buy me love. love walks right by you/movies remind you/love is missing/love is wanted/in every state/of mind.
WALKING VANILLA IS A DIFFERENT KIND OF LOVE STORY. you don't have to say you're sorry. this is a warehouse for something else. the pit of magic. the core that is always unexpected and grand. you can't plan love or magic. you can't put it on the layaway plan or order it through a Sear's catalogue. you just have to notice it when it arrives. the artist creates space for the unexpected to show up . . .
For example, the day Brett and Jacob met and fell in love was a total surprise to both of them. that's what made it so refreshing, so spontaneously unexplained. they were

both sitting in the cafe, minding their own nonchalant business; Brett was sketching and sipping mint tea; Jacob was scanning his car manual, contemplating doing a brake job on the Mercedes, when suddenly, his eyes came to a screeching halt in front of Brett's face. at that very same instant, Brett turned her pen's attention to etching Jacob's exquisite blue eyes.

Their eyes were the first parts of their bodies to fall in love. while Brett was madly scribbling Jacob's features, he took the initiative to approach her table. he sat down next to her fat thighs, though at the time he didn't notice them. he loved her smile and blonde hair and the rest of her body immediately. Brett went for his thick black moustache and narrow waist and paid little if any attention to his obviously skinny arms.

They both overlooked the other's imperfections for about four hours. long enough to fall in love, go home to Brett's apartment and intertwine all of their parts.

Then, they woke up to reality. and normal things began: disappointments/expectations/criticism/verbal assaults/physical fights/unhappiness/indigestion/heart burn and RAGE. you know, the real part of relationships.

But for four hours, they were in heaven. after that they began to get nervous and started chugging down cheap wine and chain smoking. cover-ups for the great emptiness they were both beginning to feel creep deep inside of them. they drank bottle after bottle of Almaden Chablis and smoked cigarette after cigarette because they didn't want to think about how things were changing oh so drastically between them, even though it was just the two of them that were CHANGING IT ALL!

31 I'M WRITING THIS NOVEL so that we'll all feel better when it's over. i hope i have the right idea. i stayed home from the movies tonight, thinking i did.

Buddy: discipline is important, if you want to get ahead.

Author: i had discipline tonight! i had faith! you can go to the movies any night, right?

Buddy: that's right!

Author: but how often can you write a novel? only once in a great while.

Buddy: now you're talking!

Author: maybe i should have gone to the movies.

. . .

If nobody ever said hello to you, you would begin to feel pretty peculiar. this is why the holidays are particularly hard on people who are alone; the sense of not being said hello to is terribly HEIGHTENED.

. . .

Brett: hello, Jacob. no. i can't come over. i'm just walking out the door.

Jacob: where are you going?

Brett: to a friend's house for dinner. i don't want to be late.

Jacob: drop by after dinner, o.k.?

Brett: maybe.

Jacob: call me after dinner.

Brett (getting off the hook): ok. o.k., goodbye.

. . .

Jacob is worried. lonely and creaking inside. he is afraid of rusting and freezing over for the winter. Brett is nervous and irritable. she is afraid of giving in to old impulses that fire intermittently in her heart. neither are doing so great this season. but Brett *is* moving. out of the house and into the car while Jacob remains stuck to the same chair all evening. Brett turns over the ignition and heads for Annie's. it's one of the rare times that Brett is relating to a car and Jacob is not.

Brett is determined tonight. the sauna bath helped clear things up. the fog in her brain has passed gracefully out of her head into the air. tonight she is going to have dinner with her best friend, Annie, and no man is going to get in the way of her plans. friendship and *coq au vin* are too important.

. . .

48

When Brett arrives she offers Annie the bottle of Johannisberg Riesling she brought because she knows it's Annie's favorite kind. what are friends for?

Annie: wow you sweetheart. such class! and it's chilled. we can crack it right open. you know, i can't believe you're really here.

Brett (relishing Annie's responsiveness): gee. really!

Annie: sure. i thought maybe you'd have another spontaneous collision with that wreck Moscovitz!

Brett: he's jealous. he's threatened. he is a wreck, actually. men sure don't have it easy these days.

Annie: women haven't had it easy yet.

Both women nod their heads in agreement.

Brett: hey. let's not talk about men tonight. let's open that bottle and then i want to hear all about your latest research and your program and all the women in it. i've been missing everything lately. i'm dying to know what's going on. i can't believe how hard you've been working. it's great. oh, it's been too long since we've talked about anything other than my love problems. tonight, it's just me and you.

The two women nod their heads in agreement.

Annie: well, me and you and the chickens. hey, that reminds me! i think i hear them calling from the oven.

. . .

Brett ate a moderate amount of *coq au vin* that evening. even if it is her absolutely favorite dish, she didn't need it because she was being filled up in so many other ways. in fact, she was so full and content afterwards, she had all intentions of going directly home to a good night's sleep.

However, while driving towards her house, a guilty nervous voice surfaced from inside her and made her turn right instead of left at the crossroads. contrary to her plans, Brett ended up at Jacob's front door.

Jacob: Jesus. where the hell have you been? it's midnight!

Brett: having FUN. having an inspiring talk. a delicious meal. being appreciated. that's all. not arguing. sharing my mind with a friend. things like that. you wouldn't get it . . . so, what have you been doing beside making up nasty things to say to me? (Brett wakes up from her trance.) what am i doing here anyway? don't tell me, i'm leaving.

Jacob: wait a minute, Brett. i'm sorry for jumping. i just wanted to be with you and i was worried. hey, come in. it's cold out there!

Brett: o.k., but cut the remarks, Jacob, or i'll leave. i swear i will.

Brett comes in but straight arms Jacob when he attempts to embrace her.

Brett: cool it, Jacob. let's talk instead.

Jacob: i'm sorry honey. i missed you. gee you look great tonight. how about some brandy. i got it special. actually it's cognac! i know how you love cognac.

Brett: but it's so expensive, Jake. you can't afford that.

Jacob: shit. what better way am i going to spend my money. you really do look beautiful tonight, Brett. and you had a good time. i'm really glad.

Jacob is desperately afraid of losing his girlfriend, so he is adopting extra special treatment that has won women in the past. Brett, being mildly drunk and greatly vulnerable (all her *chakras* are wide open after being in such safe, supportive territory all night) falls for his act, arms, everything.

Jacob and Brett are both subject to their long, complicated histories at a moment's notice. they dive into their roles at the drop of a hat/coat/dress/pants. shortly thereafter, they drop everything and are back in bed again. stuck together like intoxicating glue.

32 HAVE YOU EVER BEEN in therapy? now, there's a way to learn to love yourself. the characters in this novel are both in therapy. the main characters, that is. and are they doing great! they love their therapists and their therapists love each of them. they are both making terrific progress. they talk out all their deepest, darkest fears and anxieties every Tuesday afternoon in different offices, in different sections of the same town.

They both have trouble with their stomachs and their brains. they both have trouble paying for their weekly sessions. they both have trouble dealing with the circulation of pain and money. but the struggle is worth it. they sure feel relieved coming out of therapy blowing their noses and wiping their tear-stained eyes. they feel a whole lot more real and deep. Brett and Jake work through a slew of heavy material in therapy. they understand themselves, their mothers, fathers and a bunch of other people much better now. how do they feel after two years of therapy? why take the author's word for it? let's ask them directly.

Author: Brett, how do you feel?

Brett: SHITTY!

Author: why do you think you feel that way, Brett?

Brett: who do you think you are, my therapist?

Author: sorry, Brett. i was just curious. after all, you are my character! it would be helpful if i knew how you were feeling, wouldn't it?

Brett: well, i told you. shitty. why? beats me. that's your problem. you figure it out. i'll give you a clue. it's not my period and it's not a man. it's not my painting or my writing or my diet or even money. whatever it is that's missing in my life, i'm pretty sure i'll never have it.

Author: well, well. i'm sorry to hear that. sounds pretty serious. we're all sorry, Brett, since we can identify with your TRAGIC DILEMMA.

Brett: excuse me, won't you? i have to go write in my diary before i forget everything i'm feeling.

Author: quite all right, Brett. thanks for your insights even if they are a little dim. truth is always enlightening, i think. anyway. . .maybe Jacob can cheer us up. let's go talk to him a while. oh no. guess where Jacob has wound up. yes, he's taken extreme measures. doesn't look too promising in the cheerful area. Jacob's extreme need for attention lately has led him repeatedly down the stairs into the deep, dark basement. he hides out down there pouting and sulking and waiting so that people (you know who) will miss his presence on other levels. it's a pretty desperate tactic. see him over there in the corner. see him with grease all over his eyes and hands. see him hold Tuna Melitta on his lap. see him stare at the walls. see him jump when i enter the room.

Author: hi there, Jake. what's up? what are you doing in the basement? you look so cold and sad.

Jacob (he doesn't want to let on): who me? i was just down here thinking. getting a little peace and quiet. i'm fine.

I'll be formal, professional with Jacob. i'll simply ask him the same question i asked Brett and then do a cross-sexual analysis of the data.

Author: Jacob, how do you feel after two years of intensive therapy?

Jacob: none of your fucking business.

My, my. Jacob just slammed the basement door in our face. that rude so and so. and he complains about Brett's periods.

. . .

Neither of our characters seems to be getting the optimum benefit from therapy. neither is particularly cured or happy yet. Brett and Jacob walk down the street and when they run into people they say, "i'm fine," and "how are you?" and "i had a great time!" because i MAKE THEM SAY THESE THINGS. i learned these words very early (before breakfast) and i'm very attached to them. i am comfortable with them like with an old easy chair; i'm training my characters to be as relaxed around these words as i am. i am teaching them to get along with the social furniture.

When my characters get in bed, i have them say, "i love you" to each other for the same, basic reasons. i have them say "wow!" and "that feels good" and "i love you" because it sounds right. i have no idea, really, whether they love each other. beyond language that is. but we say these words in and out of books and beds, regardless. it's the subtle interior decorating of our social lives.

33 I THINK IT'S TIME for a new character. someone Jacob can talk to, get along with. someone whose chemistry he can mix with more smoothly. he's doing miserably with everyone else, so far. to be fair, the novelist is going to introduce a character that just might do the chemical trick.

The character's name is Fenmarian. Fenmarian is an ANDROGENE. that means Fenmarian is not a he or a she, but a both. sometimes we will refer to Fenmarian as her, when she is feeling particularly female, and sometimes we will refer to Fenmarian as he when the opposite is the case. more often than not, we will not refer to Fen at all because she-he is a very minor character, a very, tiny minor character indeed. Fenmarian is a flea.

. . .

Fenmarian is in the basement right now talking to Jacob. so quickly has Fen answered our prayers. Fenmarian is the only person Jacob will talk to when he's in the basement, even though Fenmarian isn't a person at all. yes, Jake is in one of those non-walking vanilla moods. he's in a stuck, stuck, down, down in the basement mood. let's see what he's saying to Fenmarian.

Jacob: i wish i were dead.

Fenmarian: why is that, Jacob?

Jacob: because everything is too difficult.

Fenmarian: oh, that's unfortunate, Jake.

Jacob: maybe if i were gay . . . life would be easier?

Fenmarian: yes, maybe it would. but i doubt it. look at me. i've been straight and i've been gay. i've been bisexual and i've been celibate. what good has it done me? none at all.

Jacob: that's true.

Fenmarian: i've done it with one and i've done it with two. i've done it alone and i've done it in crowds. in the ocean and on mountain peaks. in deep, deep valleys and in wide open spaces. in bathtubs/beds and on cold kitchen floors. i've done it early and i've done it very, very late, and what good has it done me? none at all.

Jacob: that's true.

Fenmarian (nodding her little flea head): that's true.

Jacob: do you wish you were dead ever, Fenmarian?

Fenmarian: oh sometimes i do. usually i just wish i were more alive.

Jacob: yes, i sure know what you mean.

53

Jacob wipes the tears and grease from his eyes as best he can; Fenmarian looks on compassionately. see. Jacob needed Fenmarian. everyone needs somebody they can talk to/let down around/shed tears around/be real around and around and around, even Jacob.

How did i know Jacob needed a friend? to be honest, i peeked into his notebook, where i usually find drawings of machines and schemes for designing elaborate contraptions. somehow i flipped to a page without pictures and was intrigued to find writing closely resembling a diary entry! was i surprised! i never expected something so personal in Jacob's little mechanical book. i copied it all down. here is what Jacob revealed about his emotions in between pages and pages of inventions and greasy fingerprints:

Jacob (extracted from the journal): i've been intellectually macho for most of my life. that's the only way i've learned to relate to people. now, i must drop all that. the mental control involved is awesome. i have enough of the rhetoric, but it doesn't do a damn bit of good. i'm trapped. i can't go back, not that it worked anyway. what i need is another person—a highly compatible woman to exchange mothering with, to check out feelings with. i need friendship. most of all i need to learn to love, to be HUMAN.

. . .

As you can see, it was high time for something or someone to enter Jacob's life. since i couldn't provide a compatible female partner right off the bat, i did the next best thing. i gave Jacob the friendship of the most compatible, androgenous flea in existence. and things seem to be working out delightfully so far with Jake and Fen. a whole lot more human than fooling around with car parts in the driveway.

34 Buddy: so this is what it's like to be an author?
Author: that's right.
Buddy: you just sit here all day making up people?
Author: a lot of the time i do. yes.

Buddy: doesn't that strike you as rather odd? i mean the way you just made-up that flea, for example?

Author: yes, it does actually. but what else of great import is there to do?

Buddy: get a job.

Author (ignoring Buddy's remark): yes, there are innumerable things i could do, but instead i'm writing this novel. yes. my fingers snapping, snapping along, walking with vanilla across the typewriter keyboard. the music of collaborating ideas, the rhythm of syncopated paragraphs. sailing, sailing vanilla fingers over the keys we go . . .

Buddy: vanilla fingers?

Author: that's right.

Buddy: are they like hiking boots?

Author: of course not. not in any way.

Buddy: i mean are they a concept like . . .

Author: hiking boots are not a concept. walking vanilla is a concept.

Annie walks into the cafe at this point and gently taps the author on the shoulder.

Annie: excuse me, Susan. have you seen Brett? i'm a little worried about her.

Author: oh don't worry, Annie. i have her at home resting comfortably after a hard night.

Annie: no doubt. did she hook up with Jacob after she left my house?

Author: i really don't feel i should say. i can't give away the plot to anyone who just wanders by. if you want to know, Annie, drop by her house and ask her. she's there right now. i'm sure she'd love to see you.

Annie: thanks, i think i will. by the way, who's this?

Annie practices restraint while gazing astonished at Buddy's gaudy tie and immense pot belly.

Author: this is Buddy. he's giving me professional advice.

Annie (looking on critically): oh, i see.

Author: don't worry. i'm not taking any of it. he's just diversion, get it?

Annie: i hope so. is that what Jacob is to Brett? diversion?

Author: oh no. Jacob is much more than that.

Annie: one enigma following another. i guess i'll swing by Brett's and complicate my life a little more. see you.

Buddy: it was a pleasure meeting you, Annie. lots of luck to you!!

Annie does not respond to Buddy's good wishes because she couldn't imagine what she would say. she waves goodbye to the author, the table, the cafe and the air. Buddy, of course, thinks he's included in the farewell. of course, he isn't.

. . .

Annie pulls into Brett's driveway. she goes to the door and knocks loudly. Brett comes to the door, half-naked and half-asleep.

Brett: Annie. oh god! hi. i have a hangover. come in. what a drag! this head of mine weighs a ton. (she holds a heavy load between heavy hands.)

Annie: did you spend the night with him?

Brett: well. . . i wasn't going to. yeah. i did. oh Annie, i feel so guilty. but i have to be honest with my best friend, right? i have to be able to talk to you about what's going on.

Annie: of course.

Brett: i wish i knew what was going on so i could talk about it! oh well. i guess i have to face facts. i'm obviously not ready to let go of him. he's in my blood or bones or somewhere.

Annie: hey, i understand. don't apologize. i just hate to see *you* upset all the time.

Brett: i hate to see *you* worry about me. as if you don't have enough with your dissertation to finish and teaching. . . listen, i'm working it out. i'm a grown girl, right? real change is coming. i can feel it stirring up. eventually, i'm going to make a clean break. in the meantime, let's lighten up, huh? how about some coffee? i sure could use it!

Annie: a quick cup for me; then i'm off to the library.

Brett: you're so disciplined.
Annie: keeps me out of trouble.
Brett: nothing seems to keep me out of trouble.

35 BEWARE OF OTHER VOICES than your own inner voice. beware of Scientology and Astrology and all the Ologies that whiz by you. Ologies say they know what's going on; they're on a power trip. before you know it, they'll be leading you down a crooked road and withdrawing all the money from your savings account. then, you'll really be lost. you think you are confused now, well just commit youself to an Ology and see what happens to your brain. you'll hear a pleasant whiz turn into a vicious hiss.

The important thing is to listen to your own machinery. your own VOICE AND COMPANY. your internal organs. listen to your liver/spleen/and sinuses. listen to your kidney/heart/colon and feet. not to someone's Ology.

. . .

When Jacob works on his car, and gets the motor to hum, when a car hums, when it is truly at home with itself, other people (even Brett, even i!) enjoy the sound of it. it's the same with people. when you're humming with your own internal machinery, when your body and brain motors are finely tuned, and in harmony with each other, you will make a fine contribution to the symphony of life. other people will love your hum even if they don't understand how your music is put together.

So don't model yourself after someone else's arrangement; model yourself after yourself.

. . .

Why do people smile at each other at the oddest times? like when they pass each other coming out of public bathrooms? or bump into each other in crowded elevators? who knows. but they smile and sometimes they say, "i'm sorry."

If the one you love goes bald, do your feelings change _____? how much_____? why_____?

what about teeth falling out_____ ? what about cellulite _____ ? what about car accidents and limbs falling off_____? cut off in the PRIME of your true love's life? do you love whole persons or parts of them? the sum of all their parts? do you have favorite parts? is love a geometry of parts? is it cumulative? is it related to an Ology? don't answer. it's too embarrassing; it would only be a lie.

36 PEOPLE DON'T CRY ENOUGH. people don't do a lot of things enough. examples are:
1. touch each other.
2. eat green leafy vegetables.
3. jog.
4. visit their in-laws.
5. water the plants.

From now on there will be more HAPPINESS. this is the conviction of the author in the middle of this bestseller. the author declares that from now on there will be more pot luck suppers and happiness. in this year of the monkey 1977, i dedicate this novel to my generation that is wired on strong French roast coffee and greasy pastry, hooked on booze/grass/cigarettes/various drugs and ILLUSIONS. my generation that is so beautifully candid and so searchingly lost. the generation of "what the fuck is going on?" the generation of three day relationships. the generation of loads and loads of body work, and layers and layers of consciousness raising, of alternative ways of doing everything including eating and making love. the brave, adventurous, thoroughly confused generation of cute baboons i love very, very dearly.

I dedicate the rest of this chapter to them, to silence, to dreams come true, to VANILLA and YOU.

37 SINCE WE SNUCK into Jacob's notebook, let's even out the experience quota by taking a little peek in Brett's diary while she's napping.

Brett (extracted from the diary): i was horney tonight. it wasn't that i missed Jacob or anyone else for that matter. it was just that i was HUNGRY. so i masturbated. i often am hungry. i often masturbate. it made me feel better, temporarily. but then i felt the same as before, even worse, since my solution ultimately didn't work; i was still hungry. i seem to be always wanting, wanting, and half the time i don't even know what it is that i want, but i want it so desperately, so intensely!

How can people be so calm? how can people just sit in a chair all night reading a good book and smiling pleasantly out to sea? not me. i'm too nervous. not as nervous as Jacob or the Author, but nervous nevertheless. i'm too nervous and too hungry in the evening to smile pleasantly or floss my teeth or sip herbal teas while lounging in an arm chair.

Maybe i should masturbate again? or call up Jacob? maybe i should take a walk or a bath? they all seem equal to me. what makes life so difficult is the terrible equality of all choices. i mean, do you know what would be the best thing to do? of course you don't. how could you, if i don't? dear diary, what good have you ever done me?

Do you want to know my most intimate secrets? o.k., fine. well, first of all, i'm picking my nose right now. how's that for detail? diary material of the highest quality. making decisions is a pain in the ass. that's why people pick gurus to follow so they don't go crazy trying to make the right decision. but which guru to pick??????

Maybe i should just go to sleep and skip the whole matter. sometimes, life is thoroughly exhausting.

. . .

That's the last entry in Brett's diary for that particularly interesting, though odd, evening in her life. what did she decide after all? well, since she couldn't really decide she did all of the above, just to play it safe. she masturbated (again), took a walk (a short one). returned home and called Jacob (who fortunately wasn't at home). then she took a bath (extra hot and extra long), read three and a half pages of a Carlos Castenada book, and fell asleep. oh yes, just before retiring, Brett ate two pieces of cracked wheat bread thickly coated with peanut butter and jelly, because it wasn't such an easy day.

It is interesting that masturbation should appear so

late in such an honest novel. it's such a common occur-
rence, after all, and here we are knee-deep in Chapter
Thirty-Seven and not a word about the topic. not until we
snuck into Brett's diary. picking your nose is another good
example of common material hardly ever spoken of out-
loud. subjects like these are most often found in diaries or
dreams. so are four letter words/closet problems/anything
taboo, like an essay on the size of penises. so if you have
any material like this in your brain, feel free to enter it in a
diary. it's usually safe there, unless you live with sneaks like
me!

38 BRETT IS WALKING down the dark, cold stairs
into the basement. she is going after Jacob. she
can't wait any longer. she has to find out. find out what?
she doesn't know. yet she must pursue her impulses, which
say get down, get down, get down in the basement, Brett.
get down in the basement and see what happens to your
IMPULSES.

Brett knocks assertively (not aggressively) at the basement door.

Jacob (in his most despondent voice): who is it?

Brett: it's me, Jake. i've come to talk.

Jacob: go away.

Jacob is delighted Brett has finally shown up. he has
been waiting for her. in fact, he planted himself in the basement specifically so she would notice his drastic disappear-
ance, and come after him. Jacob has decided to offset
Brett's recent independence with his own form of playing
hard to get. he's pitting his sneaky streak against Brett's
independent streak in order to win her love. he's elaborat-
ing his missing parts theory.

Buddy (whispering): but this is a secret.

Author (annoyed): of course it is.

Buddy: don't tell Brett. she's not supposed to know. it
would ruin the suspense.

. . .

Jacob: go away, Brett. (he repeats himself under
stress.) i want to be alone. it's over. you're right. there's no

use talking about anything. i'm too macho for you and that's that. our chemistry is off balance. it's all a pile of junk.

Brett: come on, Jacob. lighten up! let me in.

Brett's chemistry is more stirred up and enticed than ever with Jacob's, now that he is being so stubborn, so convincingly opposed to their reconcilation.

There is a long pause and then the sound of footsteps coming towards her. then the door opening. slowly, slowly a figure is revealed to Brett. it is Tuna Melitta, the cat, peering suspiciously through the slit in the basement door with deep, deep, deep green eyes (the deepest). Brett stares at the cat. the cat stares at Brett. Jacob stares at the wall. Fenmarian stares pleasantly at everybody. it is a very dramatic moment. Brett breaks the dramatic silence.

Brett: i didn't know you had a cat.

Jacob: is that all you can say to me?

Brett: relax, jesus. i just noticed the cat first. i mean it was at the door, wasn't it? what am i supposed to do, ignore it? of course i would mention it. its eyes are beautiful. almost as beautiful as yours, Jacob. (she is flirting with him now.)

Jacob (falling for it): o.k., o.k., forget it. just come in and close the damn door for god's sake. there's a draft in here! (pause) anyway. . .i have blue eyes and the cat's are green.

Brett: i know that. my god, what's bugging you, Jacob? you're acting like a three year old lately.

Jacob: that's because YOU DRIVE ME CRAZY! i used to be an easy-going, well-adjusted guy, until you came along and started messing with my brain. now i'm a nervous wreck. i can't even concentrate on my car half the time.

Brett: that, my dear Jacob, might be a SIGN OF GROWTH. maybe after twenty-eight oblivious years, you are finally starting to feel something, which would be a major breakthrough. that's not CRAZY, Jacob. that's what's called HUMAN.

EXTRA-LARGE, GRADE A TEARS BEGIN TO RUN

DOWN THE CHEEKS OF JACOB MOSCOVITZ. IT IS AN HISTORIC MOMENT.

Jacob: see, Brett. you always say i'm cold and unfeeling. but you have an effect on me, you really do. just look at me (he points to his waterfalls). you made me hide out in the basement. isn't that evidence enough that you get through to me?

Brett (stroking his hair): yes, darling. it is. i can feel it. i can feel your caring. maybe for the first time, a real sense of your caring. i love you, Jacob.

Jacob (burying his head in her breasts): and i love you, Brett. i'm admitting it. i'm admitting everything, and, oh God, it feels so good!!

. . .

Brett sits on Jacob's lap. the cat sits in the chair facing the happy couple. it is a lovely picture. it is a dream. dozing off in the chair in the basement with Tuna Melitta on his lap, talking to Fenmarian, Jacob has this very vulnerable dream. when he awakes, he realizes he is alone. still alone. always alone.

ALONE.

Jacob is not in the basement after all. he is still under a 1963 Mercedes Benz, holding a wrench in one hand, and a donut in the other. he is looking up at a broken axle.

Jacob (thinking): i wonder why i dreamt about being in the basement? how strange i am. how unlike me to dream about Brett. to dream about love. . .

Jacob notices that he has a crushed donut between his greasy fingers, and that there are wet puddles around his eyes and streaming down his cheeks. he continues to work on his car. he continues with greasy, tear-stained eyes and fingers to work on his car.

39 YOU DO NOT have to accomplish 13 things a day to be a meaningful person.

. . .

Brett: if i don't water the plants today, i'll feel just awful.

Jacob: if i don't replace the washers in that drippy sink, i'm a lazy bum.

YOU DO NOT HAVE TO ACCOMPLISH ANY ONE THING to be a meaningful person in my book.

SO THERE!

Buddy: that's awfully lenient of you.

Author: the generous holiday spirit has invaded my heart.

40 'TIS THE SEASON to be merry. fa la la la la. don't worry about it. you don't have to feel fa la la la la if you don't feel like it. even if it's your birthday or anniversary, you can feel icky, icky, icky instead. you can stay in bed all day. it's a gift to yourself. take it. say "thank you." don't say "i'm sorry." there are many different ways to celebrate. pick the one that suits you best.

41 FENMARIAN LOOKS INQUISITIVELY AT Jacob from the rim of a pair of dark sunglasses (miniature frames identical to Annie's). they are in the basement. it is not a dream. Jacob is sitting, greasy as ever, staring at the wall, with Tuna Melitta on his lap in the deep, dark and dank basement. nothing changes that much. Jacob is waiting for Brett to arrive. he misses her. not exactly. but he does miss SOMETHING. in the cold, dark basement, you begin to notice

SOMETHING IS MISSING.

Jacob: hey, Fen. why did you tell them i was dreaming all this?

Fenmarian: i didn't. the author did. but she had good intentions. she whisked us out of here, just briefly, and put us up there under the car for perspective. she introduced the dream element for perspective and depth perception. Jacob, it's always good to leave the basement because it's so nice to come home again!

Jacob (dryly): what's so nice about the basement?

Fenmarian: well, it's home, isn't it? there are no cracks in the ceiling. no cockroaches in the walls. we do have peace and quiet and plenty of green vegetables, don't we? we can talk about anything we want without being interrupted or criticized. nobody bothers us at all. not the author, not Buddy, not Annie! isn't that true, Jake?

Jacob: well, yes Fen, that's all perfectly true. but i'm bored.

Fenmarian: ah yes. that is a problem. but it has nothing to do with the basement, of course.

Jacob: i was hoping you wouldn't mention that.

. . .

Fenmarian is delivering a lecture on Architecture. for example, he is saying, you can get equally bored in any room in the house. the bedroom/living room/and garage are typical examples. Jacob gets bored in the garage working on his Mercedes, though he wouldn't admit it, not even to himself. Brett gets bored in the bedroom while having sex, though she won't admit to it either. people all over the globe get bored in the living room, even newly painted, paneled and totally renovated living rooms with thick, wall-to-wall red wool carpeting. right in the middle of sophisticated champagne and paté parties. yes, people get totally bored, and they won't admit it.

Therefore the fact that Jacob is bored in the basement is no big thing. BOREDOM, we have shown, has very little to do with the room it happens in. Fenmarian is sure right about that much.

. . .

The author lies down on the kitchen floor with a basketfull of fresh fruit. she does this because it is the first spontaneous thing that popped into her presently playful brain. Brett lies beside the author because she, too, is all for spontaneity tonight and wants to join the fun. so they lie on the kitchen floor and play volleyball with grapefruits. they play volleyball with oranges and apples. they play with food and laugh until their stomachs hurt. it's good clean fun, all right. it's therapeutic.

Brett is lying on the floor next to the Author and they are laughing and laughing till their stomachs feel as if they could happily burst open. Jacob is listening to all the fun from the basement below, where he is developing stomach cramps.

Jacob (thinking): that BITCH. here i am cooped up in the basement, suffering. and she's up there, being light and frivolous. well, just let her try and come down to talk with me now. just try it, either of you!

Jacob yells and yells until his voice hurts and cracks, and then he throws a grapefruit at the northeast wall. Tuna Melitta, who was cat-napping, stirs in her chair, awakened by the sound of grapefruits crashing. Fenmarian stirs in Tuna Melitta's lap, where she also has been napping. juice runs slowly and sadly down the cold, dark walls. Fenmarian pats Jacob on the shoulder very, very gently. then she whispers in his ear.

Fenmarian: now, now, Jake. things will change. don't get stuck in your grief.

Jacob: how can i relax when she's maliciously trying to demolish me, Fen?

Fenmarian: i don't think that's the case, Jake.

Jacob: just listen to all that racket upstairs.

Fenmarian: that's just fun, Jake.

Jacob: yeah, but they're doing it just to upset me!

Fenmarian: i know. fun always sounds terrible when someone else is having it and you're *not*. but really Jacob, i'm sure they're just having fun because they feel like it, not to hurt your feelings. come on. let's put on our hiking boots and walk around the basement, singing WALKING VANILLA. WALKING VANILLA. THINGS WILL CHANGE WHILE WE'RE WALKING. fa la la la la . . .

As Fenmarian calms Jacob, the laughter from the floor above gradually dies down and the lights are turned off in the kitchen. Brett returns to her diary; the Author returns to a late night cafe to write, and everything is darker and quieter and later than you think.

42 BRETT IS IN CRITICAL CONDITION at the County Hospital. a terrible place to be in critical condition. Jacob is notified immediately by an anonymous caller.

Anonymous Caller: Jacob, i'm sorry to report that Brett has been shot by an anonymous shooter while taking a harmless walk in a deep, dark tunnel. she is still alive, but not feeling very well.

Jacob: thanks for calling.

Jacob hangs up the phone and rushes to the hospital to gather more details of the disaster. he helplessly watches men and women in white coats wheel his beloved into the operating room. there are tears in his greasy eyes. Fenmarian is helping to hold Jacob upright; Jacob is shaking in his boots. he still isn't used to all the water in his eyes and all the twitches in his body, even though they are becoming regular occurrences.

Jacob: oh my God, Fen! i hope she lives.

Fenmarian: she'll live, Jacob. we'll walk around the hospital thinking positive thoughts for Brett.

Jacob (smiling through the tears): it's silly, you know, Fen? all the damn time i spend under the car, ignoring Brett or fighting with her, and now i may lose her! i'm an ass hole.

Fenmarian: everybody's an ass hole, Jacob. it's just that we don't fully realize it until someone we love begins to die.

Jacob: you're right, as usual, Fen. if she lives, things are going to be a lot different. i'm going to change. i mean *really* change! i'm going to stop working on that damn contraption all the time and start working on US, on our RELATIONSHIP. best one i've ever had. i'm going to go to my men's group more often and deal with my emotions—all of them. i'm going to be more sensitive in bed and everywhere else and i'm going to talk with her about my hang-ups. i'll tell her how beautiful she is, and how great her paintings are; i'll tell her she doesn't have fat thighs. do you think she has fat thighs, Fen?

Fenmarian: oh no. she has lovely thighs.

Jacob: the best! oh God. let her live so i can try harder to love. so i can do better than before.

. . .

Buddy: there is very little hope for Brett.

Author: now wait a minute, Buddy. nobody is going to die in my novel. how many times do i have to tell you that? i have to be on my toes every minute with you around.

The Author sits down at the nearest cafe table, turning her back and brain on Buddy, and scratches out all the gory details that have accumulated while she wasn't looking.

Author: ah! that's better. how are you doing, Brett?

Brett: a little weak, but basically great. i think i'm even thinner from all this tragedy. i may have lost five pounds since i entered the hospital. but my hair is filthy and my complexion is frightfully pale. how's Jake doing? he looked so upset. he really does care, doesn't he?

Author: yes, for the moment it seems that he does. i can't promise anything for the future, however. i'm sorry to say that's the way these modern novels are. unpredictable.

Brett: i understand. you've been kind to let Jacob love me even occasionally. historically, it's quite unusual.

Author: i do my best. and i guess i'm a dreamer. as well as a realist, of course. i'd like to see Jacob really love you, day after day, for both of your sakes. though i'm not sure it's at all possible in this case.

Brett: maybe this incident will change him?

Author (noncommitally): maybe. maybe not. the important thing is that you're doing fine, right?

Brett: oh yes. super. thanks.

Author: no blood, scratches or scars?

Brett: not a nick. you seem to have erased all of the damage.

Author: that's swell, Brett. (turning her back to Buddy) yes, i picked her up and made her walk. i'm the novelist so i can do whatever i want. i have the power of words, sentences and paragraphs. i have the power of erasers and i say nobody bleeds in this book.

Buddy: pain helps sell novels.

Author: i don't care.

Buddy: you should. you could be rich. if you let a few people stab each other, you could be a millionaire.

Author: shut up!

Buddy: a few minor characters getting stabbed wouldn't hurt anybody much.

. . .

Brett and Jacob are neatly placed in the basement, talking things over. isn't it nice? a lot better than hospital beds/white sheets/catheters/starched white nurses/yellow doctors/and buckets of red blood. the basement is like the HILTON after the COUNTY HOSPITAL.

. . .

Another inspiring reconciliation that lasts a lot longer and goes a lot deeper. look on the bright side of trying harder. it's not foolish when you're on the bright side of a reconciliation.

Brett: i missed you, Jacob.

Jacob: i missed you too, Brett. it's lonely and cold down here. very cold, Brett. i've dreamt about you every night and we were holding each other very tight and it was very warm inside.

Brett: i wrote about you in my diary every day.

Jacob: i dreamt about you every night.

Brett: i wrote about you.

Jacob: i dreamt about you.

Yes, many people repeat themselves under stress. let's leave these overwrought, well-meaning repeaters alone for awhile. everybody needs a little time alone with their lover, especially after a crisis. let's not meddle. let's let be. besides, it's good for me to get completely outside my characters from time to time, and completely into myself, which is what i'm going to do right now, beginning with yoga exercises for my back, followed by a tall glass of orange juice and B vitamins for my blood and then a long, long ride to the country for my brain.

Don't get me wrong. i'm having a ball concocting this story, though my errands are being neglected. but they can wait. they don't mind, not most of them anyway. it would be nice to find someone who'd like to wash the dishes and or the clothes, which are piled sky high, or someone inclined to make a nourishing casserole. or pick up my winter coat at the dry cleaners.

Fenmarian is a cute little bugger, isn't she? Brett and Jacob are confusing but trying a lot harder. Annie is so diligent, mysterious, and packed with common sense. Walking Vanilla can be a barrel of laughs when you put it to music. everything would be peachy keen, actually, if we could put it to music. yes, everything would be

PERFECTLY NORMAL.

PART II

43 FENMARIAN IS IN THE KITCHEN cutting up green vegetables. she is making a large salad for Jacob because Jacob hasn't been eating so well lately. he's been drinking beer, eating donuts, smoking cigarettes, and choking to death instead. Jacob never really has the time to cook, or the inclination, or the clean hands. the grease acquired from being a dedicated mechanic doesn't mix well with fresh green salads; olive oil and red wine vinegar go much better. Fenmarian has a real knack with dressings.

Fenmarian, who has impressively immaculate hands, and knows so much about balanced nutrition, wants Jake to have a good meal. so, she's cutting up carrots, celery, tomatoes, spinach and even red bell peppers which are 89 cents a pound. only the best for Fen's friends for as long as they last. she's even tossing in some sprouts and sunflower seeds for insurance. Fenmarian brings a large helping of colorful roughage directly to the front left wheel, where Jacob is busily screwing, hammering, and sweating.

Jacob: thanks, Fen. i didn't realize i was starving to death.

Fenmarian: oh i did, Jake. it's eight o'clock. you should eat more often. you work so hard.

Jacob: you're right, Fen. i'll be done with the brake job any minute now. hey, Fen, what's with Brett: she's been hanging out in her room all day. maybe you could check on her, huh? i hate to hassle her when she's in a bad mood and i'm covered with grease; it rubs her the wrong way!

Fenmarian: no problem, Jake. i was thinking of looking in on her anyway. i have so much salad leftover. i could bring her some. what do you think?

Jacob: sounds swell, Fen. Brett loves salads. they are her favorite diet item. and i wouldn't be surprised if she's dieting again, which she usually is. why that woman is constantly worrying about her figure is beyond me. (laughter) she acts pretty crazy around food, doesn't she Fen?

Fenmarian: well, Jake, we all act crazy around something.

Jacob: that's true. for sure!

Fenmarian is always sensitive to people using others for their own amusement. Fenmarian to the rescue. the perfectly androgynous, feeling flea with the ability to educate Jacob without making him angry or sad; now that's a gift. that's an asset!

. . .

Meanwhile, back in bed, Brett is writing in her diary.

Brett (from the diary): it is raining. not only is it raining but the clouds are hovering. i am lying in bed with the Tombstone Blues. the phone does not ring. no one comes to visit me. i have fat thighs. i have a pimple on my chin. and a pimple on my ass. a big one. it's hopeless. who knows what will break out next.

Jacob is a typical male. i am a typical female. so, we are getting along for a few days. what good will it do us in the long run! where is he now when i need him? of course. he's under the car. typical. can you imagine competing with a 1963 Mercedes rattletrap? it's embarrassing.

I am going to stay in bed all day unless something extraordinary happens, which it won't. i won't budge. i'm going to read the same three and a half pages of JOURNEY INTO IXTLAN again and again, and stay in bed pouting and dozing off and smoking and coughing. i don't give a damn! i'm not going to think about what errands i could have accomplished. i don't have to. i'm not going to breathe deeply. i'm not going to paint or write or brush my teeth. i am not! i am not! i am not! SO THERE.

. . .

Fenmarian walks into Brett's bedroom, unannounced.

Fenmarian: hi ya, Brett. what's cooking? (she smiles at the bedraggled blonde beauty before her.) would you like a little salad? it has red bell peppers in it.

Brett: no thanks, Fenmarian. that's sweet of you, but i'm not eating today. i have cramps.

Fenmarian: i betcha it would make you feel better. vitamins, you know, are sensational for cramps.

Brett: how do you know so much? it would not! leave me alone. who asked you to come by and bug me? you're making me cry, Fenmarian.

Fenmarian: oh, i'm sorry, Brett. i didn't mean to. i was just concerned about your health. so is Jacob. he sends his love.

Brett: well where the hell is he? (tears are destroying her vision.) we were supposed to have lunch together. we were supposed to have dinner. he's so unreliable.

Fenmarian: he's just about done with the brake job.

Brett (exasperated): if you happen to see him come up for air, you can send him my GENERAL INDIFFERENCE! now could you leave me alone; i want to sleep.

Fenmarian: certainly, Brett. i understand. if you need anything, don't hesitate to call. i'll leave the salad in the refrigerator in case you regain your appetite.

Brett (recovering her senses and focus): thanks, Fen. you are a truly fine flea.

Fenmarian flies out of Brett's quarters, giving her space. he returns to the kitchen to clean up stray carrot peels and celery butts and scour the cupboard walls. while he is working and whistling, Jacob strolls in with an empty plate and an immaculate face.

Jacob: wow! that was some salad, Fen. hit the spot! (he rubs a "spot" on his extended belly.)

Fenmarian: glad you liked it, Jake.

Jacob: how'd Brett like it?

Fenmarian: oh, she wasn't hungry.

Jacob (sly smile): see. i knew she was dieting again. starving herself to death over a few pounds. crazy woman.

Fenmarian: no. that wasn't it, Jacob. she seems upset and tired.

Jacob: is it me? i bet she's pissed off that i've been working on the brakes all night. well, what does she expect? here it is in the middle of the rainy season, and i'm supposed to drive around with half-assed brakes? whew... she thinks i enjoy this?

Fenmarian: i don't know. do you, Jake?

Jacob: are you kidding? i'd rather watch a good football game or go have a couple of beers with the guys. of course i don't enjoy it, but i have to do what's necessary for safety's sake. well, i guess i better go cheer her up. moody, moody. see ya, Fen.

44 Annie: get married, why?
Jacob: get a Ph.D., why?
Brett: go swimming at the Y, why?

. . .

WHY. WHY. WHY. these are some questions asked by the members of my generation, which statistically asks more questions than any previously recorded generation. i ask my fair share. for instance: is there anybody to talk to at three in the morning, because that's what time it is and i'm desiring conversation. knock. knock. nobody answers. because everyone is sleeping. everyone i know went to bed hours ago. except Annie, who's too busy answering historical questions to socialize. maybe i should make friends with people who stay up later? i wonder who they are? how would i go about finding them? are they listed somewhere? more questions/contributions to the statistics of a curious/ confounding generation that rushes around madly trying to figure everything out.

Brett and Jacob, typically, rush around with question marks flashing and exploding in their skulls. they can't slow down; they can't sit still. every time they do, they have an argument. for them, sitting still is deadly. they are children of the anxiety generation; it's not PERSONAL.

. . .

We are the children of the West, not the children of the East, where Buddha grew up and set a slower example. we are the children of parents who ordered Readers Digest and frozen meat pies. the children of parents who ordered electric knives/can openers/space ovens and space food. space heaters and outer space. we are the children of parents who ordered fast. fast cars/helicopters/airplanes and jets; even molecules are faster. we are the inheritors of a great deal of SPACE AND FAST.

THE INHERITORS of t.v. dinners on t.v. trays. the inheritors of drive-in hamburger stands/drive-through banks /drive-away cars. the quick snack/quick sex/quick success. the inheritors of smog/birth control pills/xerox machines/ and multiple fears. fast. fast. duplicate. duplicate. we can't slow down. we can't afford to. it's expensive living in the space age. it's hard on our systems/all of them. we can't slow down. we don't know how.

. . .

Still, Brett and Jacob and their friends in Berkeley sure do try harder to bake breads/make beautiful crafts/ pottery/music/flute sonatas and love. feathered jewelery/ beaded chains/delicate things. slow things. one-of-a-kind things. they try to counter the effects of fast with macrame and crochet. they try to counter the effects by touching each other, not so fast like their parents, but slow like their crafts.

Lacing up their hiking boots and holding hands, Brett and Jacob try to slowly get along, walking in the woods together. it makes them nervous. walks in Tilden Park, being perfectly relaxed and mellow, makes them ultimately nervous. the children of parents who taught them to keep moving/talking/asking a million questions even if you don't give a damn about the answers. the children who learned to be suspicious whenever the noise dies down.

Brett and Jacob never learned to appreciate the silence. but they're practicing. every now and again they hold hands and let go of their parents and the noise.

. . .

Never underestimate the value of going through hard times with good friends. if you went through a struggle with someone in 1977, it would be especially valuable to hold on to them, quietly, in 1978. go through the woods, and embarce in the thick green silence. find friends who will listen and talk with you, but will also be quiet and dream with you. let go of everything that is too fast. SLOW DOWN FOR YOUR FRIENDS.

45 Buddy: a moment of silence for the death of Brett. Author: stop that, Buddy. you're incurable. you know Brett is fine. i just saw her jogging at a healthy pace.

Buddy: life can change in an instant, if you let it.

Author: well it didn't and i'm not. everyone is alive and well and moving along in the middle of Walking Vanilla.

Jacob: glad to hear it. sometimes i think you keep killing off Brett and then bringing her back to life just to play with my head, as if i had endless endurance. as if i only cared about myself and had a hard shell around my heart. as if i were always in the basement or under the car and out-of-touch. it's not true. you've seen it. i have tears. large, real ones. you're a witness. i do care about Brett. whether she is dead or alive, i care about her very much. you're on a power trip with all those tricky words of yours.

Author: i am not on a power trip, Jacob. on the contrary, i am merely a vehicle for your lives. this is the gratitude i get for staying up all night telling YOUR STORY. i drive you around all night from one chapter to the next and then you yell at me; maybe i should charge you gas money.

. . .

If we don't love ourselves, what do we have? NOTHING. very little anyway. we have beer and wine and cigarettes and dope. we have tuna fish and the bank of america and graham crackers and hot chocolate. we have tears and memories and diet pepsi and the laundromat. we have turtle wax and body odors and root beer and the hiccups. we have headaches and menstrual cramps and pimples and the FEAR OF DEATH.

IF WE DON'T LOVE OURSELVES, WE HAVE ONLY DRAGGED-OUT EXISTENCE. boredom and frustration lurk around every conceivable corner. machines break down on us. we think everything's constantly after us. disaster rains down on us day after cloudy day. we have weddings/funerals/and bar mitzvahs and time/between, pretending everything is perfect just the way it is. we have to keep saying, "i'm fine," and "how are you?" it's tedious.

. . .

THERE ARE NO STARS IN THIS NOVEL, except in the sky. do the seasons affect your mood_____? do clouds hovering affect you the way they affect Brett_____? does the rain affect the number of blocks you will walk without an umbrella_____? did your mommy say that water would kill you_____? did she tell you that you couldn't walk in the rain but you could walk in the shower_____? ah yes. the screwy logic of childhood. doesn't it make your blood boil_____? doesn't it make your face rage_____?

Are you afraid? of death? of life? of your teeth falling out? of your hair falling out? of falling out: of airplanes? in your dreams? of falling out of love? in your life? of someone leaving you? or getting through to you? of growing old and flabby and life passing subtly by before your time is up? are you afraid? of bees and spiders and snakes? of other people? of yourself? WELL. DON'T BE!

It's silly. there is nothing to fear but fear itself. a famous president named Frank said that, and he knew. he was in a wheelchair and he overcame fear. you can too. you don't have to be a president to overcome things. you can be perfectly normal. just remember you're going to die eventually, so fear is a big waste of time, any day of the week. everything will either happen or not happen, so relax. take a load off. remember what Frank said from his wheelchair.

. . .

Author: do you often find your life crowded with people you don't even know?
Brett: yes. especially at cafes.
Author: do you have a party line?
Jacob: no, i like my privacy.
Author: do you like to touch other people's genitals or hands better?
Brett and Jacob: no comment.

These are odd questions designed to take your mind off your FEARS. which in their heightened form become your TERRORS. ask yourself detailed trivia whenever you feel a surge of terror coming on. ask yourself which kind of toothpaste shall i buy today? Crest or Gleam? ask yourself should i buy the regular size or the family size? mint or plain? ask yourself about detergents and t.v. programs, and which novel to read next. ask yourself about smooth and crunchy peanut butter. about steamed and sauteed vegetables. boiled and fried rice, poached and scrambled eggs. ask about meat and meatless food, filtered and unfiltered juice and leaded or unleaded gas.

These questions will keep you busy. they will keep you occupied. they will help distract you from an attack of TERROR. for awhile. Jacob and Brett distract themselves on a regular basis; they have a good grip on the terror-avoiding tools. here's an example of successfully filling up their lives with the security of concentrated distraction.

Jacob: hey, let's go have a pizza.
Brett: where should we go?
Jacob: how about Giovanni's?
Brett: great.
Jacob: loads of mushrooms.
Brett: loads! and sausage too.
Jacob: how about pepperoni instead?
Brett: fine. i love pepperoni too.

Jacob: then it's a perfect compromise. mushrooms and pepperoni it is.

Brett: right. a medium pizza.

Jacob: maybe a large. i'm pretty hungry.

Brett: and a green salad with anchovies.

Jacob: and dark beer!

Brett: i think i'm more in the mood for wine tonight.

Jacob: sure. red o.k.?

Brett: fine, we can split a carafe of Burgandy.

Jacob: oh. remind me to show you the new story i'm working on. there's one part i particularly would like feedback on.

Brett: i'd love to see it. and i've got a few poems to share with you.

Jacob: bring 'em.

Brett: isn't it nice to be getting along, Jacob?

Jacob: it's perfect.

. . .

Prefect, yes kids. but pretty boring. distraction often is to other people who are not reaping the benefits. for the time being Jacob and Brett are happy because they have distracted themselves completely and successfully. they are neither lonely nor terrified, at least not that they are aware of.

46 RECALL THE CHILD across the street. children who laugh at each other. the cruelty of small people that leaves the deep scars in big people. "hey you, fatty." "hey you, scrawny." "hey you, rotten egg." the harmless words of kids at play. remember the bad habits of youth? how easily one believed what others said about you. all the bad things. no wonder we all have such difficulty walking with vanilla. accepting compliments and digesting food. no wonder we all are so critical when smiling in mirrors. ancient voices forever reverberate in our heads. no wonder. what a wonder/we are even alive/did anyone escape?

NO. NO ONE ESCAPED. see the six year old across

the street. see him/her pouting. see his/her head hung down low. already s/he has learned to hate him/herself. s/he is an expert at self-hatred at six. her/his pals on the other side of the street are yelling to him/her. listen: "hey you, baboon!" "hey, Jacob, with the skinny, funny arms."

And on another street, a six year old girl is being badgered by her six year old sisters:

"Hey you, Brett. hey look who has fat, funny legs."

The six year old boy and girl believe every word. they are both thinking: why am i such a stupid, ugly baboon?

Aren't we a barrel of laughs. on the other side of streets, small wingless animals believe every vicious word. the pain causes Brett and Jacob to grow claws on the outside, while bleeding on the inside. words create great injuries. cruelty doesn't need much help after the age of six. it does an efficient job of crushing people directly from within after that.

Even though they are hurt/scratched/bruised to the bone, Brett and Jacob continue to try harder to talk/love/heal ancient wounds. even though they are full to the brim with errors/ulcers and hangovers, they keep attempting to make contact. it is impressive and noble when seen from this historical neighborhood angle.

. . .

This is a story that gives clues about human behavior. what are they? well, for one, most people are afraid of being rejected, so they reject others first to play it safe. it takes time, years of it, to trust people, and then it all changes in an instant, anyway. it's not easy, breathing openly.

47 CAN LAUGHTER CURE THINGS? can it cure cancer? being bored in the basement/fat thighs? skinny arms? no, of course it can't. life isn't a bowl of cherries or a barrel of laughs. life is a number of funny things, but it most certainly is not a bowl of cherries. (well, perhaps it is for three or four people.)

Most of us grow old and not so gracefully. most of us

have periodic bouts with PAIN. most of us are not in GREAT HEALTH, as much as we try or would like to be. who is? a little old lady around the block with piercing blue eyes and a green thumb. but she's a great exception. she eats grape nuts. she used to date euell gibbons. still, euell gibbons died. pretty early too. no one could cure him even if he was full of stalking nature. he died of organic, natural causes. even if we couldn't cure him we can admire his organic death.

We grow old, slowly but not as gracefully as the grape nuts collective, yet not as ungracefully as the bowery boys collective. our generation has weak knees, but we're not all bad. we still consume an impressive amount of multiple vitamins and grind our own peanut butter. rosy cheeks and charred lungs, food stamps and pinot chardonnay. welfare and great expectations.

Where are all the jobs going? down the drain. where are all the degrees going? down the drain. down. down. down. the drain. it's a clogged-up system. no wonder a lot of people are drying up. where have all the flowers gone? gone to get loaded, everyone . . .

Brett and Jacob are growing old. even characters depreciate in value. Brett has grey hairs and Jacob has wrinkles on his forehead. it's not much to notice but it's the beginning of decay. someday Jacob will be an old man with deep wrinkles. Brett will be an old woman with grey hair tied back in a conservative bun. they will both be slightly bent over. they will be fighting or making up. they will be arguing about the same old things. more or less. here is a conversation they will probably have when they are seventy-five years old . . .

Brett: Jacob, dear, you didn't care for my painting, did you?

Jacob: oh yes, dear. i did. i just thought the red was a bit much!

Brett: go to hell, Jacob.

Jacob: go to hell, dear.

. . .

Don't you wish a relationship would work? just once. really work, not just *last*. wouldn't you like to lie in bed with a half gallon of vanilla and the lover of your choice? lie back and watch sunsets slip below the horizon in velvety orange and pastel pink, while sipping brown simmering brandy and kissing wet, vanilla lips? isn't it really the simple things we all want? like deep blue eyes in a deep, brown face?

Aren't complicated things like life insurance and shopping lists and tax returns a pain in the ass? aren't they all terribly GREY? aren't you tired of GREY? aren't you tired of being half-asleep, half-awake? don't you want to invite a little technicolor into your life? a wider screen, a more brilliant perspective? wouldn't you like to lie down with a brown lover and vanilla ice cream and stereophonic sound? isn't it about time you got the SUNDAE OF YOUR DREAMS?

. . .

We all need a rest from life, temporarily. even if it's only a HAMMOCK. we all need a screen, a pillow, something to lie down on, even a straw mat. something to keep the nasty bugs away. a net. to catch ourselves. we all need our habits, even the bad ones.

. . .

Jacob: i've really got to stop smoking; i'm choking to death.

Brett: i really have to exercise more regularly. this cellulite is getting out of hand.

Characters grow old. they wear their trousers rolled. they measure out their life in French roast coffee spoons and pastry puffs. they come and go to the liquor store picking up cartons of cigarettes and six packs of beer; they come and go, come and go, growing older.

The imagination flies in and rescues the spirit from mundane facts of aging and shopping for crapola.

48 Author: Fenmarian is the most wonderful flea in the whole world and nobody cares.

Annie: I do.

Brett and Jacob: i do.

Buddy: i do too! you're over-reacting again. let's have a party for Fenmarian, and she'll see that we care. my treat.

Annie: yeah. let's have cake and ice cream and Bloody Marys!

Buddy: with ice cream and cake? that sounds pretty unconventional. why Bloody Marys?

Annie: because Fen likes them, and because she's a very unconventional flea, Buddy. just like me.

Author: so. let's make it a surprise party and when we give her gifts, tears will run down her sensitive little flea wings. let's do it! it will be adorable. we'll all feel so much better for reaching out and touching Fen with affection.

Jacob: you are so full of it. you're doing this for yourself, not Fen.

Author: come on, Jacob. don't be a drag, such a cynic.

Jacob: it's better than being a phoney.

Author (to everyone else): all of a sudden showing affection to Fen is phoney, huh? can't admit you care about Fen except in the basement, Jacob?

Jacob (defensive): what do you know about the basement? what business is it of yours? can't somebody get a little privacy around this place? get off my back, will ya?

Jacob stomps his work boots, makes a quarter turn, and returns to the underground.

. . .

49 EGOS COLLIDING LIKE STARS. they cause migraine headaches and skin eruptions. they rule public and private lives. we carry them to the mirror and to the grave. EGOS. we love Fenmarian deeply, and yet we are planning to make her happy primarily for our own pleasure, our own egos. do cats and dogs have such problems? how about jack rabbits?

The author turns her back on Buddy and heads for home. Tuna Melitta is waiting there, keeping the writer's chair deliciously warm, just like an affectionate, animated hotplate; just like a fulltime friend. Annie, Fen and Brett remain at the cafe chortling and sipping expressos. Jacob stews in the basement, below it all.

50 A LANDMARK CHAPTER. it is thrilling to have reached the fiftieth mark. this has been the Author's fiftieth chapter and the characters' 25th love affair. impressive landmarks. whenever you achieve an impressive landmark, be careful not to get stuck there. the human inclination is to stay put, but walk on instead. walk right into 1978 with a smile on your face and walking vanilla in your feet, and vim and vigor in your heart. let 1977 become a landmark. not you. you be a Mover. you get going into the fertile future.

. . .

There are several riddles in life/puzzles/tricks and games. there is monopoly, backgammon, hopscotch, and relationships. one riddle is: work hard, but not so hard you have a coronary. another riddle is: move swiftly but not so fast you trip on a banana peel at the Safeway. there are at least 1000 riddles in life to trip you up. all of them just waiting to be slipped on. the REAL trick is learning to be constructive instead of destructive, and the BIGGEST trick of all is learning le grand difference.

51 IN THE MIDST of our gala mood, Brett is nervous and wants a drink and Jacob is exhausted and wants to sleep. it's a case of cross-purposes. it has nothing to do with either of their personality profiles.

Brett (smiling anxiously): Jacob, for the holidays, i give you this egg nog (she hands him a full glass and clinks hers to his in a celebratory gesture) and my body!

Jacob (yawning): not right now, Brett, i need a nap.

Brett (hurt): o.k., fine. forget it. i'll just give you the egg nog. forget the body. i know. i'll give you good conversation instead.

Jacob: don't joke, Brett (yawn). i'm not rejecting *your* body. i'm just not in the mood. (yawn, yawn) can't i just not be in the mood once? i'm exhausted, Brett. it's

been a long day. Jesus, i must have tightened and un-
tightened a hundred nuts and bolts to figure things out. i
can hardly (yawn) keep my eyes open.

Brett (sarcastically): poor dear. all that screwing has
worn you out.

. . .

So, they lie side by side all that night, pretending to
sleep. they do not touch all through the deep, dark, dank
night, though they are aching to. Yet, it's FEAR, FEAR,
FEAR, buzzing in the air, that keeps them awake and
keeps them apart. i swear it is. it gets louder every year. i
swear it does. we ain't so "loose" as we say we are; we
ain't so "liberated" and free as we pretend to be. walking
down the street, smiling openly, fear builds and cracks in
our heads and we go to pieces. believe me, i have terrific
hearing, and i know the fear is louder between the sexes
than it has ever been.

Well, who isn't afraid? who isn't burnt-out or, at
least, singed by experience? who isn't ill-at-ease in the
face of love, the love of a face? you know who. FENMAR-
IAN. the most petite character in the novel.

Brett and Jacob are under the illusion that they are
getting rid of fear a little bit each Tuesday, faithfully at-
tending their Consciousness-Raising Therapy Sessions
and doing their HOMEWORK. they pay a lot to be under
this illusion. they have a lot of homework — an intricate
series of touching exercises, that keep them up late at
night. they are trying to learn to trust other human beings
with their FINGERS. you have to stay up for nights and
nights and nights practicing with every appendage available, and still it doesn't do much good.

Still, it is better to have a strong commitment to an
expensive, exhausting illusion than to give up entirely
and settle for humdrum despair. without their fingers,
Brett and Jacob would really be depressed. if they
weren't at least trying to reach out, they might even be
TERRIFIED. it's healthy to believe things will get better
even if they never will.

. . .

Brett is beating the couch with a tennis racket. it is the healthy way to kill off her father, symbolically. a clever inventive method for releasing large chunks of rage in a short session. she learned it one Tuesday afternoon when she opened up an inspiring aspect of her psychic pain. the horizons of her emotions have broadened immeasurably and her awareness thickened impressively, since she has been alloting Tuesday afternoons to ACTING OUT. it has only cost $275 for Brett to kill her father with a racket so far . . .

Brett: it's worth it, but i wish it would stop hurting!

Barton: it hurts me more than it hurts you, dear.

Brett: yes, Daddy. yes, Daddy (crying): stop hitting me, Daddy. it hurts, Daddy. i'm sorry. i'm sorry. i'll never do it again.

Author: wake up, Brett. wake up. it's o.k.

Brett: i must have been dreaming.

Author: yes, Brett. you were dreaming of your father. you said Daddy several times. i got that much.

Brett: it was awful!

Author: yes. sounds like a nightmare. do you think you can remember it for your therapist on Tuesday?

Brett: i can try. i'll write it in my diary.

Author: good thinking. it will save me some paper work. thanks, Brett. and don't be too upset. i'm sure some wonderful insights will come from this dreadful experience.

. . .

Jacob just comforted Brett after she retold her vicious dream. "poor honey," "mean daddy" and so on were some of the phrases Jacob used to calm his jangled girlfriend's nerves.

Buddy: excuse me, you two. but i was wondering what you are doing on New Year's Eve?

Jacob: i have no idea.

Brett: heard of any parties?

Buddy: parties? no. quite honestly, i haven't. but why don't you two go to the Phoenician Room like my wife Edith and i do every year. what a ball we have! it is only forty-eight dollars a couple for an entire evening of dining and dancing.

Jacob (to Brett): get a load of him. do you think we have that kind of money? we're not in your bracket, Buddy. he sure doesn't pay attention, huh, Brett?

Brett: only when he wants to.

Jacob (to Buddy): if we spend ten dollars *together* on New Year's, that will be extravagant. more than we can afford. right, Brett?

Brett: right, dear.

. . .

It's fun to get along even if it's at somebody else's expense. enemies, like Buddy, are useful when couples don't get along. enemies like Buddy are excellent distraction. walking off into the sunset, holding romantic hands, Brett and Jacob discuss the innumerable obnoxious characteristics of professionals instead of focusing on any of their own vast differences.

Brett: what a creep!

Jacob: the Phoenician Room! do you believe it?

Brett: forty-eight dollars!

Jacob: we'll have more fun with a bottle of cheap champagne. champagne is always great, even the cheap stuff.

Brett: right, dear. maybe a little egg nog too. imagine dancing cheek to cheek next to a bunch of Buddys in tuxedos!

Jacob: hey, honey. let's stay home together on New Year's Eve, light a fire and practice with our fingers until the sun comes up!

Brett: sounds perfect!

They kiss/hug/laugh their heads off. they are in love. they hate Buddy. Happy New Year, Buddy! you just assisted Brett and Jacob in making up their minds about New Year's Eve.

. . .

Jacob is swearing at nuts and bolts. he does this instead of hitting a couch with a tennis racket. in his own way, his own symbolic way, he, too, is knocking off his parents with the tools he likes best.

. . .

Jacob: it's cheaper than therapy. that's for sure.

Author (puzzled): but i though you *were* in therapy?

Jacob: i'm experimenting with it. just going a few times to see. not like Brett. i'm not going to make a *career* out of it.

Author: neither is she Jacob. it's not her vocation, you know. she's an artist like you.

Jacob: if you ask me, what she needs is more hobbies. things to keep her hands busy with something other than pastry. (Jacob laughs uproariously.)

Author: can i light your cigarette, Jake?

Jacob (putting a Lucky Strike between his lips): hey, thanks.

The author strikes a match and ignites Jacob's thin, white extension. looking slyly at the smoker, she watches Jacob inhale deeply.

Author: i guess all your activity with nuts and bolts doesn't curb your oral fixations?

Jacob (in between choking on large drags): hey, cool it. i can QUIT ANYTIME I WANT TO!

Jacob storms off smoking inside and out; a smokestack; an angry young man.

. . .

While Jacob and the Author are arguing, Brett has returned to her diary, a warm quiet place where nobody yells or criticizes or misunderstands her intentions. she is happy and far away from fights. so far she doesn't even hear the muffled voice of Jacob hollering anymore. she writes her current, quiet revelations in her little, green book.

Brett (from the diary): Annie says that women lovers are the most intimate relationship there is. i wonder if she's right? can't know unless you try, i suppose . . . does it follow that relationships between men are the least intimate?

I know that when i hold my women friends close to my heart, there is HARMONY i've never experienced with men. some women say it's far better to hold men close and pay attention to the dramatic, puzzling, tense DIFFERENCE. sometimes i even feel this way. vive la difference, i whisper, imagining April in Paris. leave it to the French to come up with romantic bullshit. then again, Americans haven't done badly on that score either.

It probably has more to do with family than country origins. all my life i've been trained by Gloria and Barton to feel this way. to pursue the international prince, all decked out in white suits, white tennis shorts, and white cadillacs. just so he's rich and charming and respectable and *white*. just so i get married by the time i'm thirty, they'll be happy. time is running out. what does all this mean? does any of it have to do with happiness? with intimacy? with ME?

Who knows what intimacy is anyway? i know i'm certainly not prepared to measure it. maybe Annie is? maybe someday someone will invent a machine that measures intimacy between people, so we'll know for sure who's suited to who. it's possible in this highly refined technological age we are all heirs to. an evolved form of computer dating with a single, wonderfully clear variable: INTIMACY.

I know very little about love between males and females, or between females and females, or between males and males. it's all quite illusive to me. the only thing i know about love is between houseplants, and as far as i can tell, houseplants are bisexual.

P.S. dear silent, polite, no-feedback diary of mine: WHAT IS IT I WANT SO BAD THAT I SHALL NEVER HAVE? (no answer.) i figured as much. well, it's not a dishwasher or a color t.v.

52 THERE ARE INNUMERABLE DOORS in the world, and we always want to open them, even the rusted ones. the ones that creak, and stick and scare us to death. the ones that lead into darkness and the ones that lead nowhere. you can't tell a door by its handle. when you successfully get one open, there is often another directly behind it. i can't open your door for you, and you can't open mine for me. occasionally, we can hold doors open for each other, and that's about it.

There are never enough windows.

Annie, a real door-opener, now enters Brett's kitchen door, after peeking in the kitchen window. she is not a voyeur; she's just a concerned citizen.

Annie: hi. i just saw Jacob and Fen at the zoo. i thought he was baking bread with you today?

Brett: well, he was. he did. he left to see the penguins. you know how he is on the weekends.

Annie (bewildered): huh?

Brett: well, you know. he likes to take Fen places. it's sort of like having a son. they go to matinees, the zoo, car races, the five-and-dime. things like that.

Annie: are you covering for him?

Brett: God no. of course not. what's wrong with it if a guy wants to take a flea friend to the zoo on a sunny day?

Annie: it's overcast and damp outside.

Brett: well, it might clear up.

Annie: i doubt it . . . not for a long time.

Brett: what do you think of my breads, Annie?

Annie: they are beautiful.

Brett: one is for you. pick one!

Annie: i'll take this one. it's got the most poppy seeds. i adore poppy seeds!

Brett: no kidding! you do. oh i'm so glad. i was worried people might not go for them.

Annie: hey, listen. i got a brainstorm. as long as Jacob and Fen are frolicking elsewhere, why don't you and i go have a holiday drink at Brennan's? Irish Coffees on me!

Brett: yeah, sure! why not (she thinks for a moment to see if there is a reason to lock herself in for this day, but luckily doesn't find one). sure. i've put in a good day baking and i'm all done! no reason to stick around.

Annie: you deserve a break.

Brett: yeah, an Irish Coffee break!

Annie: i'll drive.

Brett: you're a lifesaver again. your timing is perfect.

So they are off and running to the friendly neighborhood pub.

. . .

They are so many different reflections. notice how differently one appears depending on who they are with. sometimes one friend is a better mirror for you than another. it's identical with glass. just when you're convinced by one mirror that you are fat, along comes another pane to point out how slim you are, in fact. clearly. just when you've grown accustomed to the paleness in one mirror, you gaze in another and discover your health has miraculously returned. which mirror is true? which friend reflects us best? with all the people and mirrors in the world, it's tough figuring out what you're really like, isn't it? take a look at Brett bouncing her image back and forth between Annie and Jacob. foggy to clear. foggy to clear. then, there's always the big family mirror of Mom and Dad, which is usually cracked down the center.

. . .

Rooms are plentiful but homes are rare.

. . .

Annie and Brett *are* having a great time (not just a good one) sipping Irish Coffees, engaging in deep dialogue while surrounded by boisterous young men whom they don't notice at all. they are too involved and happy to be bothered by anything, even whistling and snide comments that stroll by.

. . .

Buddy: aren't any of you girls going to get married? isn't anyone going to settle down and have a baby?

53 MEANWHILE, Jacob is chasing Brett all over town, even though he ran away first. it happens every day to the peculiar creatures of this earth. it happens to the stars in this novel/on every planet/between all the elements that are immensely attracted to each other and immensely repelled. who choreographed this jolting dance?

Those not participating, sit out and watch the parade pass them by. SOME OF THE MOST BEAUTIFUL BODIES SLEEP ALONE. Brett often sleeps alone with her fat thighs. stroking them sadly, she thinks: it's good no one is here to endure the touch of these over-stuffed limbs. and Jacob sleeps alone, thinking how small he is in comparison. to what? to something much larger, more substantial. to a dream he has tucked away in the warmer folds of his colder heart.

Brett and Jacob sleep alone and they dream of each other. when they sleep together, they dream of other people, or they dream of sleeping alone. it's typical. they are swimming in a dream pool reaching out . . . the breast stroke, the backstroke, the crawl. they awake early. they awake thirsty. hungry. hung over. they don't understand what they are doing in the same bed. when they are miles apart in their dreams. it's common. the very quiet war between sexes/bodies/brains/souls. even the best couples in the whole world split apart like atoms; it's the powerful age of anxiety.

the split inside.

the split outside.

FEAR: a stream running through the middle of us like the San Andreas Fault. it shakes things up. it brings people to dinner in winter. most people adore acquaintances being propelled into their living rooms during the winter, though they often find it distracting during other seasons.

Brett is thinking wintery thoughts while half-blitzed at Brennan's.

Brett (thinking): it would be nice if Jacob and i got along. we could build a fire and sip brandy. we could snuggle up. it's warmer (sometimes) when he's beside me.

Jacob (thinking equally romantic thoughts while rushing around in the rain): i blew it again. i just don't know how to act. i can't expect her to wait around for me to fly in and out. i wish i could find her and we could build a fire and drink brandy. what a perfect day to stay in bed with Brett and snuggle up.

Neither of them knows the other is thinking such compatible thoughts. if they did, they too could be having a great time together.

54 BRETT AND JACOB ARE BACK in bed together, returning once again to the familiar. the same old story, they are having a great time. just listen:

Brett: i love you, Jacob.

Jacob: i love you, Brett.

They are in bed together, behaving in an extremely friendly and familiar manner, so i am having them say these words. i love you. i love you. i love you. ohhhhh, i love you.

They are going to have an orgasm (perhaps a couple) any minute now, so i am going to leave them alone by ending this chapter early and giving them complete privacy and total satisfaction. i'll just close the door on this chapter and let them have as many healthy orgasms as they like.

55 THE CHARACTERS HAD A GREAT TIME. now they are hanging out in the kitchen munching leftover croissants and drinking freshly perked French roast coffee. it's Tuesday. life begins again and again. the cycles of love turn/as the laundry turns/as the world turns. the characters experience AFTERGLOW. the reunited feeling.

Here is an up-to-date account of Jacob and Brett's thoughts while standing naked in the kitchen, munching/kissing and lying through their teeth.

Jacob: this will never last.

Brett: this might last.

Jacob: i need her.

Brett: i needed that!

Jacob: Fenmarian will be pleased.

Brett: Annie thinks he's a pig.

Jacob: she's too much into Women's Lib stuff lately.

Brett: we should take more hikes together. we need to be more active.

Jacob: i'm hungry. it's winter and i'm freezing to death.

Brett: i'm hungry. it's winter and i'm freezing to death.

Author: they're hungry. it's winter and they are both chilled to the bone. standing in the warm, afterglow kitchen they experience the inevitable draft.

56 BRETT AND JACOB ARE HUNGRY and it is winter. so they are trying harder, extra-hard. they are talking and talking and talking it over, while the soup gets cold and the nights get darker.

Brett: you've been spending a lot of time with the Author lately, haven't you Jacob?

Jacob (defensively): i'm one of the main characters, aren't i? i've got to discuss things with her from time to time.

Brett: you're a liar, Jacob. i'm a main character too; you've been sleeping with her, haven't you?

Jacob: i have no idea.

Brett: what kind of answer is that?

Jacob: it is the ONLY RATIONAL ANSWER. i'm only a character. i have no idea. if the Author wants to say we slept together, we did. if she says we didn't, we didn't. simple as that. i'll see you later. i've just been instructed to go back under my car.

Jacob exits. Brett remains standing, partially nude, partially shocked. she screams after him.

Brett: you SON-OF-A-BITCH. you smart ass. when am i ever going to get a straight answer out of you? (softer voice, to herself) why do i waste my time with that idiot?

. . .

Because it's winter. because of the hunger/that cannot be filled/because it's cold/and we have dreams/of creating warmth/out of TENDERNESS/for the Holidays, at least.

. . .

94

LONELINESS IS AMERICA'S NUMBER ONE KILLER. if you've got it, try to wipe it out. writing replaces the need for sex, but not the BASIC HUNGER. the hunger is replaced by . . . WHAT? i have no idea. i sound like Jacob. characters rub off on you. his language is getting to me.

You can't always find a lover. so if there isn't anything decent in the near vicinity, get a stuffed animal.

Annie: they're often the same thing.

Author: that's funny; funny and true. Annie. hey, that was some fight Brett and Jacob just had?

Annie: the same old story.

Author: yes. what is it, Annie? what went wrong with our generation?

Annie: did anything go wrong?

Author: well, didn't it? all this confusion, fighting and excess!

Annie: maybe things are just getting right, better anyway. look at it that way. things just look worse because we're paying attention. you know, like when someone decides to take care of their health, suddenly they recognize a million little illnesses, areas that need improvement. well, now that we're questioning certain relationships, we are noticing the lack of communication, sexism, patriarchal violence, *little things* like that!

Author: maybe we're all too heady . . . maybe we'd be happier as farmers? do you think you'd be happier on a kibbutz in Israel? a friend of mine wrote me this week from there; says she's happy, skinny (she used to be a tub) and healthy picking dates. could that be that answer? are DATES the answer?

Annie: who knows? maybe for her. what do we know from way over here. it's only a letter, after all.

Author: how true. only an aerogram, a thin piece of onionskin. maybe she's a BIG, FAT LIAR.

Annie: for her sake, i hope she's telling the truth. me, i'd get bored picking fruit. i've got to use my head, which reminds me . . .

Author: i know, off to the library.

Annie: not this time. the Post Office, actually. sorry, Susan, you usually know where i'm going.

Author: oh i'm glad to be surprised now and again. and while you're there you can mail this aerogram for me.

Annie: to your skinny, happy date-picker?

Author: yes, though that remains to be seen. she'll be moving back next month and we'll get a closer look.

Annie: if she's so happy in Israel, why is she moving back?

Author: MONEY and PARENTS.

Annie: ah yes. two of the most powerful movers in the universe. 1000 times more powerful than Bekins.

. . .

What about you out there? do you see hope for your life? do you see travel? what are you going to change next? your underwear? linens? lovers? attitudes? addresses? you can't help but change something. don't resist it. RESISTANCE IS PAIN. let go. move it!

Take a look at Annie swinging down the street to the Post Office. she has vitality even doing everyday errands. observe the way she looks interestedly in shop windows and smiles directly in passing faces. what a HEALTHY ATTITUDE. WHAT A MOVER.

57 I'M DRIVING DOWN Shattuck Avenue thinking about my characters. i'm obsessed. i admit it. they are driving behind me/beside me/on top of me/and all around me. Jacob, why are you following me in that crummy Mercedes? Brett, riding shotgun, madly scribbling in that diary of yours. Of course, Fenmarian, delicately perched on my shoulder, singing song after melodious song. Annie's in the backseat, telling me we'd all be better off if we ditched Jacob and got on with our HERSTORY.

ALL MY CHARACTERS ARE HAUNTING ME. instead of thinking of friends, like a normal person, i focus on plots and subplots. what about Brett? does she have a hangover? did Jacob really sleep with the Author? did Fen ever get her birthday cake? even a plain old pound cake? i'm even worried about Tuna Melitta, who drives me nuts jumping up on my lap to see what's doing in my novel (even though she really doesn't enjoy reading). still, i've become attached to that crazy cat. that's how committed i am, to the development of a bunch of neurotic characters. i'm a sentimental fool.

Annie (leaning forward from the backseat): you know something. we could put our energies together and accomplish something in this book. Sisterhood is Powerful! we could overcome a great deal in a few chapters . . . a little editing.

Author (curious): what do you suggest, Annie?

Annie: well, first off, i think we ought to cross-out this skinny guy driving behind us in that rattletrap. he's not worth it and he keeps taking us off the track. why not erase him?

Author: because he's here. because Brett is working a lot out with him, and because there is HOPE.

Annie (leaning back in disgust): oh Christ. it goes on and on. Tuesday through Friday. the Author sees HOPE? i often feel pretty lonely in this novel. sometimes i feel like getting out.

Author: come on, Annie. it's not so bad. we're friends. you and Brett are getting so close. Fen adores you. everyone does actually except Jacob and that's only because *you* hate *him*.

Annie: drop me off at the library. i've had it for one day. i'm suffocating.

Annie curls up like a cocoon in the backseat, turning off her senses until dropped off at the library. armor is important and Annie knows how to let it up and down at the right times. like a car window it is a survival tool, adjusting the quality of oxygen coming through slits in your life.

Buddy: gee. i like Annie. we all do. she has beautiful eyes, the prettiest i've ever seen. i just don't know why you girls are so self-defeating? you should take your own advice. a good attitude makes all the difference in the world.

Author: connections make a difference.

Buddy: they are *both* important. that's true. they go hand-in-hand. with a good connection or two and a good attitude, you're going to be a very, happy young lady.

Author (playing devil's advocate): oh yeah? look at Virginia Woolf. all those wonderful books, and fame, and was she happy?

Buddy (innocently): i imagine she was. yes, she was quite successful.

Author: sorry, Buddy. your imagination stinks. she was not happy. she was miserable, in fact. being a success is not the whole picture.

Buddy: that doesn't sound like such a good attitude.

Author: it's easy to be critical, Buddy. you're a white male with advantages. you're rich and don't have to write this novel, so your back doesn't constantly hurt. it's easy for you to talk about good attitudes in a five-hundred dollar suit.

Buddy: my back does too hurt.

. . .

My characters follow me everywhere i go, even Buddy, in his expensive, sleek Lincoln Continental. they are like children; i understand them like a mother. we have a strong SYMBIOTIC RELATIONSHIP.

I am like a mother who takes the girls to girl scouts, and the boys to boy scouts and everybody to the Orthodontist. only my characters are grown now, so i take Annie to the Library, Jacob to the Auto Parts Store, and Brett to her Dance Workshop. i don't mind; it's good to get outside the novel with a drive down Shattuck Avenue. it's good outside if it's not pouring rain or freezing snow and you have a good winter coat and a friend to meet. otherwise, i recommend you stay indoors. there's a lot of colds going around this season (there always are) and special flu bugs (there always are). so . . . stay inside. stay warm/light a fire/invite a good book or person into your arms.

58 THERE WERE FIVE TIMES more instances of cancer in 1977 than in 1976. why are we DYING OF OURSELVES? What good is Ecology doing us? how do we go on living? even the sea is dropping dead. is it possible to WALK WITH VANILLA, knowing all this?

. . .

Can perfectly normal types, like Brett and Jacob, counteract all the corruptible forces that go on in the world with their ambiguous love?

. . .

Starvation/cruelty/unemployment go on. despair/fat deposits and suicide go on, but wait. DON'T JUMP. there is hope. there are free and fabulous things in the world nobody pays enough attention to. uncontaminated things. so PAY ATTENTION. Brett and Jacob, artists with little money, you are prime candidates for free things. pay attention to Solar Energy (it's free); pay attention to each other (love is free); pay attention to yourself (you can be free). Freedom is Health and Health is Precious; it is a Light at the center of your life. LIGHT IT UP! light it up and see if something better doesn't go on.

. . .

Brett started growing sprouts this week. it's a beginning. Jacob is working at the Recycling Center on weekends. it's another beginning. small beginning grow into tall oak trees. foot by foot across the great American Vanilla Desert, you can be an acorn stepping out to save the forest of America. you can save your skin/life/friends. so whatever you do, don't GO OFF. STAY ON. depression causes acne, water retention, and who knows, maybe it causes CANCER TOO.

59 DURING THE HOLIDAYS, many people take airplanes to visit relatives they don't understand/can't talk to/and would rather not be around. It's the holiday spirit.
People show adoration by traveling very far to eat

turkey, cranberry sauce and mince meat pie. to drink egg nog, brandy and alka seltzer. people spend a tidy sum they often don't have on air fare and Christmas gifts. people clench their teeth and "have a great time." it's expensive; people get pretty full and pretty empty this time of year.

Both Brett and Jacob's families live in the Bay Area (at least they saved air fare). they had to have Christmas dinner twice in one day because they weren't prepared to play favorites, which is a dangerous occupation with relatives *and* holidays. here is an excerpt from the first dinner at Brett's parents' sprawling mansion:

Brett: um, this is delicious, Mom. you really did it this year!

Jacob: yes, Mrs. Starr. really terrific. wow!

Gloria: well, thank you, dears. i'm so glad you're pleased.

Barton: how was the trip down?

Jacob and Brett (in unison): perfect. no traffic at all!

The young couple laugh together, feigning amusement at having said the same thing at the same time, though in fact they are just releasing nervous tension.

Gloria: how pleasant. won't you have another portion of my dressing, Jacob?

Jacob: oh thank you, Mrs. Starr. it's wonderful. i just can't stop eating it.

Brett: me either, Mom. this is my third helping!

Barton: not much traffic, you say? good to hear. the roads have been dreadful lately. so many "types" moving out to the suburbs. isn't that right, Gloria?

Gloria: right, Barton, all sorts!

Brett (uncomfortable, wanting to change the subject): well, i'm full, Mom, you'll just have to give me this new recipe. it's the best ever.

Gloria: oh yes, darling! it's in *Suburban Corner.* they have the yummiest recipes ever. they do such nice things with spices, don't they, Barton? i've been using it for all our parties, right, dear?

Barton: that's right, Gloria. what was that dish you

surprised me with last week? a kind of bouillabaisse. oh boy, was that an extravaganza of flavors! i sure love that seafood; how about you, Jake, like lobster?

Jacob: oh yes, Mr. Starr. i sure do.

Gloria: we've been eating fish more than red meat now that you read all this about nitrates and cholestrol. right, Barton?

Barton: that's right, dear. we stay fit and healthy around this house.

Barton touches his middle to indicate trimness. Gloria, likewise, is fatless. she doesn't exercise. she just uses generous portions of saccharin in her black coffee and only eats one slice of French bread when they dine out. she has discipline and stays a beautiful woman because she loves her handsome husband.

Everyone smiles at The Starr Residence. a fortunate family full of rich food. everyone except Gloria is aware of bellies pushing against laps. everyone is a little miserable and lonely and nobody lets on. after all, it is the HOLIDAY SPIRIT.

. . .

And here is a bit of conversation lifted from the second dinner at Jacob's parents' comfortable brown shingle, family style home.

Sy: so kids, how was the drive over?

Brett and Jacob: perfect. very little traffic.

Vy: so, Brett. would you care for a little more of my stuffing? It's packed with chestnuts, you know!

Brett: oh yes. it is delicious. you'll just have to give me the recipe, Mrs. Moscovitz.

And so on . . .

Families are often unsettling; we go anyway. they mean well. that's why we go anyway. they have our best interests at heart. even when they are stuffing us full of carbohydrates. what Brett and Jacob need after Christmas is a massage/a sauna and a laxative. they could also use a little peace and quiet. people give and give and give during the holidays and get very little back. is that possible? where does the love/energy/holiday spirit go????

. . .

Brett gained five pounds during the holidays. all in her thighs. this is what she had to say about it:

Brett: that god damn dressing—a shit load of carbos!

And this is what Jacob had to say:

Jacob: all this holiday crap has put me days behind in my schedule.

Brett: what schedule this time, Mr. Machine?

Jacob: i can do without your sarcasm, Brett. i'd like to finish the valve job so maybe we could take that trip to the country we keep talking about. talk is cheap, you know. action is what counts.

Brett: cool it, Jacob. i'm telling you. i don't like your mouth lately. *it's cheap.*

Jacob: fine, i won't talk. you go worry about your thighs and i'll work on the car. that way we're sure not to have an argument.

Brett: suits me fine. go play with your implements. you never listen, anyway. you're a brick wall.

Jacob: thanks for the support, kiddo. you are cement loading me down.

Jacob heads for his playpen, which is the garage, and Brett visits her favorite sounding board, which is Annie.

. . .

Brett: you were right. he's insensitive to me. no matter how close we get, as soon as he doesn't like the way things are going, he climbs back under the car.

Annie: they always find something to hide under or behind when something REAL comes up.

Brett: i see it all now. i can't change that lunkhead. i'm going to shift my focus; start doing some hiding myself! like behind my easel and behind my typewriter and my STRENGTH.

Annie: that's talking!

Brett: to hell with him. i'm making a new year's resolution! you're a witness, Annie.

Annie: i'm all ears.

Brett: from now on my creative self comes first. his mechanical self comes first for him, so it's only fair.

Annie: sounds more than fair.

Brett: yes, my health comes first too. no more getting blotto and ruining my work time.

Annie: looks like the holidays are doing you good.

Brett: hey, Annie, what did you do Christmas day? i've been so wrapped up in my resolutions, i forgot to ask.

Annie: not much. didn't feel like celebrating.

Brett: did you stay home? oh yes . . . i could have invited you to my mother's. she would have loved it. i've been so preoccupied. what a friend . . .

Annie: lighten up. you've been fine. i know i can come to you. if i'd needed to be with you on Christmas, i would have said something.

Brett: really? sure? even so, i should have asked. i never get to help you.

Annie: you'll have plenty of opportunity to come to *my* rescue, believe me. like after my dissertation is done i just may collapse in your arms from total exhaustion. anyway, friends don't MEASURE!

Annie leans against Brett's shoulder (practicing) and Brett instinctively strokes her hair (she's practicing too). Brett thinks: this is the finest friend i've ever had.

Annie thinks: i love her. sometimes it hurts to touch. but it's the wrong time. i can't say anything. she wouldn't be able to deal with it now.

Brett thinks: i should pay attention more. i should be worthy of her. from now on i will follow my heart instead of my gonads.

They both think: i am lucky. we are equals. a treasure has entered my life in her/her.

60 BE CAREFUL with images. there are many ways to say be careful and so many ways to say i'm sorry, and usually nobody listens anyway. there are an infinite number of angles to shoot from/boundless images/and countless people—only a few cameras. there is time. not

much, but a noticeable amount. film is expensive. images are cheap. be careful sandwiching your talent between cheap thrills/strange people/time/space and white bread.
. . .

Buddy: i happen to be very interested in the imaginative side of the brain.

Author: is that so? i wonder if it's interested in you!

Buddy: i went to art school for two years. but i had six sisters and brothers. we didn't have enough money for artists in the family. i had to go to work. (he frowns.)

Author: we don't have time to tell your story too, Buddy. i'm sorry, but we have our hands full already. i'm sure it's a very touching story, but it will have to wait for another novel.

Buddy: oh i don't mind; that's about it, anyway.

Author (reflecting in her sentimental fashion): hey, Buddy, remember kissing cousins? and footprints in the sand?

Buddy: ah yes, hey, will there be any footnotes in this novel?

Author (knitting her brow): i don't see what for. why do you ask?

Buddy: just curious. it's always good to know things. it helps business go more smoothly.

Author: business never goes smoothly for me, with or without footnotes.

61 FENMARIAN IS DOING her laundry. she owns two tee-shirts, one crisp white one, and one deep blue as the sea. a scrumptious pair of corduroy pants which are red, but not blood red, and a cool, silk blouse which is green, though not as green as Tuna Melitta's eyes. Fen also has a Vanilla Overcoat.

Fenmarian is so easy to be with, even when she's doing something as mundane as the laundry. she is delightful; she is as comforting and deep as the ocean. listen to her do her laundry on the Banks of the Ohio, on the silver-streaked rivers of Mexico, Italy, Greece and Spain. listen to her rocking the laundry in Portugal, Morocco and Israel. on the rocks by the River Nile, the Amazon and the Erie Canal. she makes beautiful music and 8 by 10 glossies on the Uljas-satori River in Mongolia, her laundry romantically tossing in the wind above the red sea, black sea and mint-green sea; Fen gets around. she has a lot of dirty laundry, and tremendous motivation to clean things up. rocking with her clean sheets and shirts, smiling radiantly out to sea, Fen-marian is the most beautiful flower swaying in the cool, Vanilla breeze.

62 ALL THE CHARACTERS are hungry; only Fen seems to have small needs in comparison. is this because she is so small? no. it is not as simple as all that. she's a big giver; in fact, in proportion to how small she is, logarith-mically, she gives 1000 times her weight in filling up others. for example, today she made lunch for everyone in the novel. it wasn't an ordeal. it was a delight. that's how light and giving Fen is. and can you imagine, she wasn't just whistling while she worked, she was actually YODELING.

Author: i'm full. Fenmarian made her special spaghetti sauce and it was so delicious i couldn't resist. i ate the whole thing!

Brett: i ate too much.

Jacob: i ate too fast.

Fenmarian: i ate just the right amount for me.

Annie: i wasn't hungry. i was finishing my lecture for Friday.

Buddy: i wasn't invited so i had a pastrami sandwich on a Kaiser roll at the Delicatessen. oh yes, and an Egg Cream and a piece of pie.

Author: what kind of pie?

Buddy: apple.

Author: perfect! you and apple pie. how American, Buddy. hey, don't you ever worry about your weight, or at least, cholesterol?

Buddy (defensive): i watch my weight. but nobody's perfect. i just felt like a piece of pie today. can't hurt once in a while.

Author: i'm sorry, Buddy. i forgot how hard you try,

even though it doesn't show. many things people try don't show immediately. not for a long, long time, if ever in fact.

. . .

Everyone was hungry and everyone got fed, except one little character who was left out though not on purpose. Fen doesn't leave people or animals or insects out on purpose. But Tuna Melitta was in the basement and didn't speak up or meow. by the time she smelled the sweet essence of oregano and tomato paste coming through the floorboards, she felt too rejected to even purr softly for attention.

Jacob has come down into the basement carrying a half-empty beer can. pasta makes him drowsy. he's going to take a nap. as he collapses on the cot, Tuna Melitta nudges up to his nose and speaks:

Tuna Melitta: when are you going to feed *me,* Jacob?

Jacob (genuinely concerned): gee, Tuna. i'm sorry. i've been so preoccupied with my own hunger and everyone else's, i honestly forgot about yours. there's so much hunger, it's hard to keep track of it all. hey, Tuna, what would you like for lunch?

Tuna (pouting): i want a large green salad, and i want Fenmarian to make it for me!

Jacob (stroking Tuna's upturned, angry fur, trying to be patient): now, now, Tuna. we can't take advantage of that cute little flea, can we? she does too much for us all as it is.

Tuna: sometimes i think you love Fenmarian more than any of your friends.

Jacob: Fenmarian *is* one of my closest friends, Tuna.

Tuna: what about me?

Jacob: i love you, too, Tuna. very much. and i feel badly about your hunger.

Tuna (hiding her cat face in her paws): i don't believe it.

Jacob: well, it's true, sweety. would i let you sit on my lap if i didn't care, huh?

Tuna: sure you would, out of pity.

Jacob: i am not into pity. i am not into rescuing people

and animals. i am not! i am not! why does everyone keep accusing me of things i'm not into. (beginning to lose his temper, Jacob delivers a lecture on his attributes.) i am not a pig, i am not out to ruin Brett's creative energy. dig this, Tuna. she calls me up at eight this morning—woke me up—to inform me of her BIG DISCOVERY. (actually, Jacob called her, deeply lonely for her company, but he lies about it even to Tuna because he is embarrassed to admit that his manhood is becoming a shell of its former self.) apparently, i siphon off her creative juices. i'll tell you something, Tuna. that Annie creep is brainwashing her. i swear she is. she says that now that she's seeing me less she's doing more. poem after poem! painting after painting! swell. who cares. what does she think i want? all her time? hell, no.

I want time alone, too! i want to write all those unfinished poems in my drawer. i never get anything done when we're fighting either. i still have so much work to do on the Mercedes and in the yard. the plumbing in the house and the refinishing job on my chest. shit, i'd like to build a bookcase, do i ever get the chance? hell no.

She wants time alone (shrugging his skinny shoulders) she should talk. (to himself): i want to be with her. if i only had what i had before, i'd really appreciate it. now i'm bored. i sit for hours in the basement, shaking. last night, i called up three men from my group. see if they wanted to go to a movie, play cards, anything. they were all involved with something else. nobody cares about me anymore. (to Tuna): i'm a hell of a lot busier than her!

Tuna (trying to console Jake, who's become overwrought): that's right, Jake. i hear you!

Jacob: thank God someone does. let her paint all year. let her have a million shows in galleries. let her travel, what the hell do i care? relationships are impossible anyway. the sooner i admit that and get back to work, the better off i'll be.

Tuna: that's right, Jake. you show her!

Jacob (touched by Tuna's support): Tuna, i'm really sorry i yelled at you. my nerves are frayed.

107

Tuna: that's o.k., Jake. i understand. hey Jake, you make me lunch. Jacob, YOU TAKE CARE OF ME.

Jacob and Tuna Melitta embrace. it is a tender moment. it's as good as the movies. as moving as James Dean nursing his dad in *East of Eden*. Jacob gets along better with fleas and cats than women. strange but true. a tear runs down his eye, or is it grease? whatever it is, it's REAL. Jacob knows how to be real around animals and cars and some houseplants, but not around Brett. will he ever be natural around the opposite sex? WILL BEING THE OPPOSITE SEX EVER BE NATURAL FOR HIM? will the cloud that suspensefully hangs between men and women ever pass? will Brett and Jacob bridge the almighty gap? can people stay full between meals? kisses? love affairs? jobs? is there a simple antidote for emptiness beyond breakfast, lunch and dinner? do snacks help? will hunger bring us together or tear us asunder?

Jacob leans on Tuna Melitta for the moment, and cries like a baby because nobody ever loved him enough, and because he's had to cover himself with grease in order to conceal the deep, deep scars of childhood games. Jacob drops his John Wayne facade because for a brief moment he trusts his cat friend enough to expose every raw nerve in his body. he is naked before the very deep, deep, deep green eyes of Tuna Melitta.

63 MEANWHILE, Brett is restless. she is riding her honeycombed horse over tall, white fences into deep, green woods. she is riding high with Vanilla. restless, but free, her blonde honey hair whips the wind and brushes her face. Jacob enters her mind from the left side; it is a painful entry. Brett is thinking: i am horney.

It is a dream. yes, yet another one. Brett has her fair share of odd dreams too; yes. everyone does.

Fenmarian is riding on Brett's shoulder. smiling all the colors of the rainbow into endless blue sky and Brett's end-less blue eyes. Fenmarian relates so well to the sky, as well as everything and everyone else. it's hard to believe it's a dream. it's so vivid when Fen's around, even in your sleep.

Fenmarian is pleased that Brett has gotten out of the

house and up on her horse and is riding in Vanilla wavey dreams. Fen can tell this form of exercise is good for Brett. he can tell by the vivid color in her cheeks. color is an important indicator of people's health and state of mind; so is the lack of it.

This technicolor dream with stereophonic sound indicates that Brett's health is returning to superb at a rather rapid and impressive rate. it's about time/everything is.

Fenmarian as usual is walking easily and exquisitely with Vanilla, reverberating like a shimmering star on the backdrop of the world. it's so textured and splendid to see Fen move through the blue of Brett's dream, we ought to snap it and make it permanent. yes, let's blow it up and give Fen her own image as a birthday gift. a giant size Fenmarian poster.

Buddy: hey. we could make a couple hundred and send them out as holiday cards.

Author: no, no, Buddy. that's too commercial. i wouldn't do that to Fen. we'll just make two or three special prints and give them to intimate friends. sweet little postcards of Fen and Vanilla walking across the sky in a variegated dream.

64 DID YOU GUESS that between pages and pages of research Annie had time to keep a journal? well, it's true. and it is also true that bad habits *are* habit-forming, because this writer has become an avid reader of other people's secrets. so, shall we sneak???

. . .

Annie (journal entry): it's a great relief to be intimate. still, sometimes it frightens me. i know. there is nothing to be afraid of. i know it is an illusion that i will break apart, and yet, when love arrives, often i don't know how to behave.

With men it was easy, cool. instructions swam through my mind like how to tie shoelaces, how to ride a bicycle, how to apply for a job. the methodology women practice all our lives. . .we can go through the steps with our eyes closed.

How to hook a man: pull a big one out of the sea. take

him home to bed with thee! wrestle and squirm in the waves of separate passion. alone, thrashing about in the same bed. performing a ritual we have slick models for, and putting on a good act. i'm done with that!

So many women have learned to live with the absence of something immense years ago, they don't know anymore what's missing. they've accepted those holes will not be filled. i can't accept those limitations; it would drive me crazy if i did.

Making love like that is like going nowhere for a short while. like having a cocktail at the airport lounge. in between flights. a floating space/film/a cartoon. playing at love in a series of reruns. keeps this industry going. the BIG SHOW. it does no harm, except it makes us liars. no harm except it wastes our precious lives!

. . .

Brett and Annie are having dinner together in a special cafe. they are eating mushroom quiche and spinach salad and sipping chilled chablis. they are eating and talking and touching hands/minds and hearts. talk about full!

Brett: it's so good to be together.

Annie: it always is.

Brett: things are going so much better with Jacob. really, Annie. you wouldn't believe it. he's really changing.

Annie (nodding and smiling): if it feels good to you, i'm happy for you.

. . .

Later that same night Annie is moved to write more in her journal. there's a lot going on in her brain, as you may have noticed! it's as if her love for Brett has suddenly come to a head in her head.

Annie (in the journal): our eyes are like mirrors. i see myself in her. a window into my own soul. our eyes are more honest, i think, than our lips. our lips are clever but not always honest.

There are a million things i don't say to her. no, that's not it. really only one thing. one difficult thing. perhaps she too doesn't say these words to ensure their non-existence. i wonder what she "names" the feelings that pass between us? could i really be alone in what i am experiencing?

Women speak of the men in their lives, and the names roll off tongues like honey. Brett and i can speak of our work and smoothly, easily, we agree on strategies. yet, there is much fear between us. words stick in my throat.

Does love between women hurt less?

It shouldn't be this way between women, i wanted to shout at her. WHAT TO DO WITH THE LOVE I AM NOT SHARING . . .

Maybe there is no Jacob between us, not really. maybe between women there are sometimes the names of men we make up to protect us from the intensity of our love. maybe MEN ARE WALLS THAT HIDE US FROM THE PASSION DEEPLY BURIED IN OUR SPIRITS.

I would like to face this openly with Brett. i would like to say simply and directly, without putting names between us: i really love you, Brett. i want to say it and stop the lies that come between us.

And yet, i don't want to get caught up in romantic images and ruin everything. i love what is REAL between us and i don't want to lose that. and my work is going so well; even though there is pressure, it's quality stuff.

What does Jacob give her beyond illusions? fantasies? i want to know. i hunger for that knowledge almost as much as i hunger for Brett and my Ph.D. i'm obsessed with seeking out the meaning of their relationship, and keep coming up with empty answers. it seems he's got no substance, and still causes great damage. it's screwy. i am furious that men rip off beauty like layers of skin.

I am angry at myself for talking to a journal, instead of to Brett! i feel deceptive and dishonest. the chapter i just finished stinks.

Hey, Oakhurst, don't get all depressed. let's practice a little of that positive attitude stuff you're always throwing around! sure. i enjoy spending time alone more than i ever have. it's wonderful being at home with myself. it would be nice to share, but there's time. it *will* come. tomorrow i've got a great luncheon and tennis match to look forward to, and books and books to cover before i sleep. not so bad. actually, with a little editing the new chapter has great potential.

65 Brett (entry in her diary): why do i still settle for so little in men compared to my women friends? i've been brainwashed. if i don't seriously begin to change, i will get permanently locked into habits that have chained my mother to my father. i must pull up roots and replant my HERSTORY and let it grow. Annie has been a great inspiration. her brain is full of good fertilizer.

Why is it Jacob always shows up when i'm feeling flat? why couldn't he come around when i'm in a creative fit? why couldn't he come in horney as hell while i'm painting my masterpiece, so i could splash oils in his face and be done with him at last?

i'm hungry. i should be. i've been painting all day without a break. what i need now is Protein. what i deserve and can't afford, but am going to buy anyway is PORK CHOPS. i love pork chops, and God damn it, i'm buying two of them (big ones). i know if i was with Jake tonight, he'd talk me out of it. "let's economize," he'd say. "we can't afford it," he'd complain. i know him. he'd say, "come on, Brett, let's eat pasta instead." and i'd listen to the idiot! not today. i'm settling for nothing less than what i want. sometimes it's really thrilling to be all on one's own.

. . .

Brett throws down her diary. throws on her coat. throws open the door and throws back her hair. Brett heads for the local supermarket. she's in a throwing things around mood, as you must have noticed, including her hips. her behavior is probably due to the fact that she has been standing in the same square foot for five and a half hours, painting a still-life. she needs to shake things up. the blood in her veins, the laughter in her belly/the song in her heart.

. . .

Annie (behind sunglasses where she is hiding tears and secrets): here we go again. (to the author): couldn't you leave them apart for a minute? Brett was working so hard in her studio. you've ruined it.

Author: i didn't exactly mean this to happen. really, Annie. i just sent them both to the market. because they were both hungry for dinner, and both their refrigerators were empty, which is typical and believable for artists, right? i can't help it if they bumped into each other at the meat counter, can i?

Annie: you sent them there. one of them could have ordered out.

Author: come on, Annie. don't pick. it's not my fault they shopped at the same supermarket, at the exact same time and both decided on pork chops. how was i to know there was a sale on pork chops at the Coop.

Annie: so now what?

Author: well, now one thing leads to another. they decided to bread their chops together. and split a bottle of zinfandel, and it's a cold night, of course, and they are hungry/horney and who else is available to either of them on the spot? so there you are and here they are.

Annie: it won't last.

Author: oh, i know that by now. but it is fun watching how things fall apart, isn't it?

Annie: you sound like Buddy. *no, it's not!* i'm going to the library. if Brett and Jacob fighting is your idea of fun, please don't invite me to any of your parties.

. . .

Brett and Jacob are in bed after a filling meal, so filling they have no room for sex. hungers can be transformed and transferred instantaneously and inconspicuously by a couple of pork chops and a bottle of wine. they don't mind the loss of sexual appetite. they are enjoying lounging comfortably in bed together, having a friendly, intimate chat.

Brett: that was great wine, hon. you really know how to pick 'em.

Jacob: i love the way you FRY those pork chops, honey bun. god, i missed you this week. seems like a lifetime.

Brett (snuggling up to Jacob's warm, right armpit): Jacob. have i ever told you that you have the most beautiful eyes in the Western Hemisphere?

Jacob (blushing): oh come on, really? guess what i love most about *you?*

Brett: what?

Jacob: you have to guess (playfully): come on! three guesses!

Brett: my hair?

Jacob: nope.

Brett: my mind?

Jacob: nope.

Brett: oh, i don't know. my eyes? come on, what is it?

Jacob: your thighs.

Brett (irritated): shit, Jacob. do you have to tease me?

Jacob: damn it, i'm not. i love your thighs. i know, i know. you always complain how fat they are. but i'm always thinking: gee, Brett's thighs are so earthy, sexy. i mean WOMANLY. oh sweetheart, i wish i could convince you.

Brett (disbelieving): how could anyone really love these trunks? (Brett clasps her legs and tears come immediately to her eyes. as if they were squeezed all the way up from her thighs into her face, as if Brett's thighs were the bottom of the tube and by pressing hard with her fingers the toothpaste has come all the way up through her eyelids.)

Jacob (bringing Brett closer to him, hugging and whispering): oh Brett, baby. don't be so hard on yourself. i love you. you're beautiful. i love you.

Brett: i love you too. do you believe it, Jake?

Jacob: sometimes i do. lately, i wonder myself. lying here with you, i feel secure. you're so much softer when we make love and are away from the world. it's nasty and cold and hard out there. sometimes in cafes/parties and supermarkets i hardly know you.

Brett: yes. i know what you mean. i feel the same way when you're under the car or in the basement. only in bed do i really feel your love, feel i know you.

Jacob: maybe we should stay here for a few days and build up our confidence?

. . .

Another brief vacation from grief and pain. a nice picture to recall when it's Winter and it's cold and you are all alone, which you usually are.

. . .

For a while, our young couple was perfectly happy, a happiness that lasted all through the night and all through the house. a happiness that came smiling into the daylight. to kiss them good morning!

Yes, the next morning Brett and Jacob were thoroughly APPRECIATIVE. they made love and they laughed. they bounced up and down in bed like a happy cowboy and cowgirl. they let go. they WALKED WITH VANILLA in bed all morning long. then they made the bed and brushed their teeth and smiled in the mirror, satisfied with what they saw for a change!

They jumped up on their bikes and rode to the Mediterraneum Cafe, where they had cappuccinos and croissants. they held hands and smiled. they glanced at the morning paper. they felt like pals. they felt not alone. they felt FULL. it was a simple, open feeling, and a relatively inexpensive morning (seventy-five cents each).

. . .

THE EARTH IS TURNING. some of its characters are falling off the edge/with fear/with disgust/with technology/ with California. bodies falling into cold/violent green-waters. holidays falling/life falling/love falling/failing/turn-ing/the earth/falling into the Pacific Ocean. some of my friends are falling off the EDGE/of this/NOVEL. not me. i'm a writer. i'm committed. to finishing/before falling/off/i'm responsible.

it's perfectly normal. it's
perfect.   ly.   norm.   al.

Fenmarian died. Buddy stepped on her with his brand new, shiny, brown PENNY LOAFERS.

PART III

66 DOING IT THE AMERICAN WAY puts a great strain on the kidneys and other vital organs. the boozed-up liver and the smoked-up lungs. just listen to everyone coughing (choke! choke!).

Still, people can be luminescent hexagons revolving in the sun. many-sided human beings with many-sided potentials. it's a fluorescent picture if you see it that way; it's an optimistic tube. turn it on!

PRACTICE THE EASTERN WAY OF DOING THINGS: a little bit of bliss goes a long way. in the midst of capitalistic chaos, every minute of taking care of your own hexagon is commendable; it's geometrically sane. so! . . .

Do sit-ups at the HYATT REGENCY HOTEL. do hatha yoga deep breathing at DENNY'S, transcendental meditation in the alley between two federal BANKS. do Tai-Chi in the SAFEWAY parking lot. levitate your spirit at JACK-IN-THE-BOX. bring the west and the east together. save your ORGANS. SAVE AMERICA. save your KARMA and a friend's. happy new year. reflect your self-love in the great outdoors. share. say OM. say anything that feels good.

live in the wide open spaces of your heart and the fertile fields of people. love is a small, wingless animal with tiny, pleasant reverberations. you have to stop, look and listen to feel its baby grand repercussions: don't be afraid to slow down and hear the emptiness curling inside you. having a hole in the middle of your musical spirit is quite common. in fact, it is shared by everyone. like a gunshot wound, we are all metaphorically shot full of holes. you are not alone. contrary to common belief, you are TOTALLY SURROUNDED.

67 THIS NOVEL COVERS a lot of ground. it flavors the whole earth with VANILLA. you can take it to bed with you and feel at home with all the weird entries under the covers. you'll never feel totally alone or totally odd if you have a copy by your side.

This novel is singing in the moonlight/through the trees late at night/it is dancing across the ocean/it is dreaming on the edge/it is falling/into your hands.

. . .

Everyone has forgotten about Fenmarian who died a few pages back; how lightly we take the death of others. how heavy our own appears to us.

68 BRETT IS DANCING in front of the living room mirror. she is twisting and twirling in the delightful afternoon sunlight. she is thinking: i am a special person; i have supple long legs. i have written two good poems this week, and i'm getting along marvelously with Jacob. also, the lighting this afternoon is quite flattering. nothing could be better. life is perfect!

Watch out. this is a dangerous way to be thinking. to accumulate such snotty, arrogant ideas in her brain today might just get Brett into trouble. sure enough. she just broke out in pimples on her unsuspecting chin and a cloud just passed over perfect sunlight. you can't stay perfect (no one can) for more than a moment or two at a time.

Recently, Jacob created a perfect (tenuous) situation

for himself. moments later his battery died. the constant build up and breakdown. the process we are all prone to, sitting up or lying down.

Jacob yells at indifferent gods, temporarily forgetting that everything is perfect just the way it is. fifty dollars later, things are back to normal, sort of. Brett temporarily covers up her flaws with Clearasil and rain clouds go on their merry way.

While Brett and Jacob are pretending life is perfect again, life continues boxing them from the left and from the right, but it doesn't knock them out entirely; they're still too young for that.

. . .

Brett and Jacob, two young, free and easy artists, put schedules around their lives like fences. they need to pin themselves in. to pretend that other people take away their freedom, when in fact they do it to themselves. fear motivates them. fear of what? nobody knows, exactly. yet everyone agrees it's pretty SCARY.

Brett and Jacob have built a sturdy fence around themselves to keep fear out. they have their own private, detailed list of activities and errands to keep them preoccupied. they complain about not having any free time, but that's just a trick people play on themselves to feel important. if they had the extra time they pray for, they would be even more FREAKED OUT than they are already. it's typical. it's the American way to appear meaningful and keep the strings together.

Yes, even artists who sit in cafes like Brett and Jacob do all day have their own particular habits, package of patterns, and predictable pathways to keep them safe and secure.

For Brett and Jacob, "hanging out" is serious, part-time work. they occupy three or four cafes in town during the week, and each one has a precise function in their enterprises. one is for morning coffee and croissant and newspaper. a second is for inexpensive hot luncheons and snacks and late afternoon beers. a third is for rewriting manuscripts, sketching and staring at walls. and the fourth, which has a deck overlooking the Bay, is for voyeurism, gossiping with friends and getting a suntan.

It's all highly structured. don't kid yourself. if you observed Brett and Jacob for a week, you'd discover their obvious schedules and be able to find them day or night; even artists are not unique. even artists are deathly afraid of FREEDOM.

. . .

There's nothing to be afraid of in this novel. nobody has died or bled, right? so don't be afraid if you're involved with the characters. love them to death. you're not going to lose them. just an occasional pimple or dead battery, nothing to get scared about. . . we may not be cured in this novel, but we sure are getting better, aren't we? we sure are getting ripe?

. . .

A lot of closets have opened up lately. it makes life easier to breathe. open a few closets on your own. see if life isn't less stuffy for you and your pals.

. . .

If you rub up against someone like a feather, instead of a fist, you will surprisingly enough feel a lot more. Brett and Jacob learned this in a sexuality workshop weekend. now, when they are in bed, they try to remember to be light as feathers, instead of hard as rocks.

. . .

What kind of fences surround you? are you in the mood to tear any down? or were you thinking of building a brick wall around your heart? which way are you walking this year? OR IS IT POSSIBLE THAT YOU ARE

DANCING??!!

69 A PERFECT SCENE: wine glasses glittering. candlelight glowing. Brett and Jacob wrapped in classical music and velvet clothes. a Turkey wrapped in aluminum foil. stuffing sweetly surrounding and inhabiting the luscious beast, resting on a silver platter. Cranberry Sauce nearby. houseplants, green uppers climbing all over the walls, inhaling the clean, sweet air. the Holidays. New Year's Eve. Kisses/Plum Pudding/Hard Sauce/Soft Smiles /Beginnings. everything is perfect and perfectly placed.

Jacob: you look beautiful this evening, Brett. i love you.

Brett: you are so handsome in your blue velvet shirt.

Jacob: your green dress is a knock-out. who needs money. when you've got love and Value Village to shop for clothes.

Brett: yes, Jake. i thoroughly enjoyed picking this dress out of a pile of rags. discovering it among the rubble. it was like . . . KARMA. and only one dollar and fifty cents. honestly, i enjoyed it more than buying a brand new two hundred dollar dress at I. Magnin's.

Jacob: i know what you mean, Brett. our integrity intact and our love. i feel together. whole. and we are growing so much. i can feel my *chakras* opening up. (he points to his chest to indicate opening.)

Brett: you know, Jake. when we get money, *we'll* know how to spend it. we won't corrupt it. we'll enjoy life, right?

Jacob: to the hilt, darling. shall we toast, then. to a prosperous and healthy (maybe wealthy?!) new year!

Brett: and to you!

Jacob: to us!

The clink of celebrating champagne glasses resounds through the rooms. Brett and Jacob love each other back and forth all evening. like a healthy tennis match, they volley their strong emotions back and forth from nine until two in the morning, and that's about it. why? because people don't really know how to keep it up. they just know how to Serve and Perform extra specially well on romantic occasions like New Year's Eve. all the trimmings help. especially three bottles of champagne.

Brett: HAPPY NEW YEAR, JACOB.

Jacob: HAPPY NEW YEAR, BRETT.

. . .

They are wearing party hats and sipping party drinks. they are making plans for a glorious future. it's high class, holiday pretending. it's the irresistible spirit.

Perennially, HUNGER wakes them, whets their appetites. HUNGER is so many-layered, it is thicker than the thickest LASAGNA. thicker than the floors of the WORLD TRADE CENTER. the varieties of human hunger, piled on top of each other, pierce through the BIG TOP of the American sky and go way, way beyond.

Thus, Brett and Jacob continue to try to get along. they are characters with long myths/histories and underwear. still they are freezing for love. i've put them on earth to tell this story. i have told them to love each other and they are doing the best they can. they are doing pretty damn well, too, considering all the obstacles i've put along their path to enlightenment, like Brett's fat thighs/frustration with art/money and men and Jacob's car which is a rattletrap and his lack of tools/for dealing with relationships.

Jacob(addressing the Author, sadly looking at her with tear-stained, greasy eyes): will it ever end?

Author: no. not for a long time, Jacob.

. . .

Brett and Jacob are in a cafe—the fourth one—the one for gossiping and staring at walls. they are doing a little of each right now. sitting across from Buddy and me, they are alternately smiling adoringly, squeezing hands lovingly and lighting cigarettes effectively. while Jacob is thinking about his carburetor, Brett is thinking about Tampax.

Jacob: how are your cramps, honey?

Brett: better, Jacob, thanks.

They are adorable. they are good actors. they really know how to act in cafes. to whisper and giggle and puff together. they are EXPERTS in cafes or at home accompanied by champagne. still, 50% of their energy is almost always somewhere else, lost in the jungle of their separate thick heads.

Brett and Jacob are still artists who see life in extremes. if you put on a pair of glasses that were mirrors of Brett's and Jacob's brains, you would see most of the world in dialectics and dichotomies; you would have very wide lenses and see the farthest extremes on the horizon. because that's how Brett and Jacob perceive things. yet, though they have very, very sensitive vision, they often don't have very wide perspective. all the extremes tend to blur the middle where one usually has to function. all the extremes tend to tip them and trip them and bruise their (blind) little hearts.

70 FENMARIAN CAN SEE EVERYTHING. no use trying to hide your feelings or blemishes; it won't work. you're in her field of vision, which is very wide, indeed.

71 THERE ARE A LOT of odd jobs and artists have to do them in order to keep moving, not to mention to keep the roof over their heads. SURVIVAL IS STILL AN ISSUE. jobs are still a critical issue. there are fewer and fewer jobs (meaningful or otherwise). does this mean there is less and less survival?

Jacob works as a d.j. even though he'd rather write a novel. Brett works as a bread baker, even though she'd rather paint and write poems. both Brett and Jacob resent their jobs and also feel fortunate to have them, considering the scarcity.

Fenmarian doesn't have to work. Fenmarian is on Welfare. Fenmarian is unemployable. Fenmarian is disabled. Fenmarian is so small no one will hire her; it's SIZEISM. it's serious. it is an issue totally ignored by CONGRESS.

Buddy: hold your horses. i was led to believe the poor, little flea had died. fell off the edge of the novel or the world awhile back. by the way, the insinuation that i might have crushed her with my shoe is preposterous!

Author: it's not so preposterous at all, Buddy. you almost did crush her, but you were oblivious to the fact on account of rushing off to some business conference. anyway, i caught her in the nick of time. i pretended she died for suspense.

Buddy: i thought you were an honest novelist. i thought you didn't pretend.

Author: everyone pretends, Buddy. no one is perfect. even honest novelists tell fibs. no one could stand Fenmarian dying. it was too sad and pointless, besides i did promise. i may be a fibber but i always keep my promises.

Artists are a part of the economy even if other people, including the government, act like they aren't. even if doctors act like they don't have stomachs or teeth. it's not true. artists have G.I. tracts and cars that break down; Jacob has his battery problem today. tomorrow. . .maybe a radiator. Brett needs her front tooth recapped; she broke it on the kitchen floor during a fit with Johnny Walker; and you should see the pile of bills on my desk!

Artists don't escape the machinery. it's still a question of survival 95% of the time. a question of constantly repairing one's personal and impersonal contraptions.

Artists don't get what they deserve, except three per cent, who haven't shown up yet. hey, if you're out there, rich artists, could you drop us a line? if you're so damned rich, why not a telegram? we'd love to hear from you in any form. sincerely, the rest of us.

. . .

THERE IS TOO MUCH MONEY IN THE WORLD.
THERE IS TOO MUCH A LACK OF IT.

72 JACOB AND BRETT have been getting along for a whole day and a half, in so many different places and so many different ways. not just in bed but in cafes (all four of them), even in the late low blood sugar afternoon while shopping for dinner. even later while getting caught in a nasty traffic jam on University Avenue. Jacob got a parking ticket while they were in the Coop Market and STILL they continued to get along.

See how much they've changed and mellowed out? see how much less spoiled/rotten/tainted they are since they began really communicating and trying harder? see how helpful friends like Annie and Fenmarian have been?

Brett and Jacob are having their LAST SUPPER together. not in any religious sense, only in the Novel sense. there's nothing unique about it, except they are prepared to chew everything, together. today, they are trusting. it's just like family; what's not to trust?

They kiss. they cook. they digest it all. they light a fire and sip brandy. they sit in a Morris Chair in the comfortable silence. then, Jacob speaks:

Jacob: Brett, honey . . . there's something i've wanted to ask you about . . . ah ah, i've been hesitant, cause, well i thought you might blow up . . .

Brett (remaining calm and relaxing on the trusty diagonal): nowwwww, Jacob. you should not be afraid to talk to me about *anything* that comes to mind. that's the only way our relationship can mean a thing, if we are open and honest. then we will grow!

Jacob wants to be straightforward; he tries shaking his body out to release its twitches.

Jacob: wellll. it's sort of about Annie. i mean about you and Annie. i mean it has nothing to do with the fact that she doesn't like me.

Brett (irritated): Jacob . . .

Jacob: o.k., maybe it does. and maybe it's both of us that create the tension . . . (he looks to Brett for approval and she gives him a nod, which allows his tremors to reduce and he continues, though he is sweating profusely beneath his overalls). well. not that it matters or *would* matter to me, it's just that i wondered if you and Annie ever . . .

Brett (knowing what he's getting at but refusing to help him out): if we ever what, Jake?

Jacob: you know (he mumbles it) got it on.

Brett (returning to the sobering vertical): listen! there is something i want to get clear with you. things have changed for me and you'd better know it, Jacob Moscovitz. i've learned incredible things about myself and my own life. no. to answer your question, Annie and i are not lovers...though who knows, Jake. we may well be some-day. i'm open to that. i'm open to a number of things these days.

we are close. i love and respect her. she treats me with kindness and support. we share many things, Jacob. she's important in my life. you cannot fill the spaces she does. and i'm not going to make any promises or place any limitations on my life for you/for anyone.

Jacob (defensively): HEY. i wasn't asking you to.

Brett: o.k., maybe you weren't, Jacob. but i'm covering my bases. you *have* asked things like that of me be-fore...i'm not your pushover girlfriend-appendage any-more, or your mother, or your child, or...

Jacob (angry): god damn i know that.

Brett (interrupting): wait a minute! (she drills words right through his resistant head.) i'm beginning to see *my worth* as a person, as an artist. neither you or i have given me much credit. so get off my back for how i lead my life. you've tried to fuck it up enough already.

Jacob: ease up, huh. i don't want to chain you down. i think you're the greatest.

Brett: don't soft soap me! o.k., sex with us has been great. big deal. (tears come with her shouting.) I AM AL—MOST TWENTY-NINE YEARS OLD, JACOB. FUCKING ISN'T ENOUGH. i want more than occasional, passionate moments. i want a partner in life, a companion. a support system. not someone who periodically comes up from under a car to kiss me to death.

Jacob: hey wait a minute. i love you! you should know that by now. i'm not dating anyone else.

Brett: that's not it, idiot. and to hell with the words. I LOVE YOU. I LOVE YOU. big deal. show me, Jake. act like a loving person, that's what counts. anyway, i'm taking care of myself this year. that's my New Year's resolution. i come first. i've got paintings to paint and poems to write and songs to sing! i've got friendships to explore and Jacob i want to dance more. i love to dance. why don't i dance anymore? because i've been too upset. too drained. too crippled. I'M GOING TO DANCE, JAKE.

Jacob: wonderful. so dance!

126

Brett: i'm not going to waste my precious energy arguing over nothing with you, anymore. i'm beCOMing and anything that stands in my way, goes.

Jacob: i'm becoming too.

Brett: so great. we can both be free to grow.

Jacob: i want more too, Brett. (frightened): i want us to last. (he is thinking about losing Brett to Annie, and he shudders. Jacob is trying to save himself from drowning in the sea of love. lately his body is a rattletrap from all the stress. it's hard to handle.) i'll try harder, Brett. i'm sorry about Annie. i admit i'm jealous . . .it's natural, isn't it? but whatever you need, GOES. that's right. but i really want us to be together. i mean really TOGETHER. i want a companion too. not just a sex partner. that gets so old. i'm almost twenty-nine too! i'm tired of playing around. maybe we should do more things together. go to plays. i bet i can get some tickets. maybe we should go to Mt. Tamalpais soon and hike, and have a picnic. be quiet and peaceful. be alone together. it's so beautiful up there. we've never gone, have we?

Brett: no, we haven't.

Jacob is crying. tears are running like a river. he doesn't try to stop them, he merely diverts them to one or the other side of his face with the back of his hand.

Jacob: i want to go beautiful places with you, Brett. because you are such a beautiful person. i don't mean your face or your body, i mean inside, honey. and i want to make you happy, Brett.

Jacob falls forward with emotion and lands horizontally in the rocking chair of Brett's shoulder as she remains relatively calm and erect while rocking him.

Brett: i have to make me happy, Jacob. (softer): but you can share your own happiness with me. we can share, Jake.

Brett is giving a brilliant performance at the LAST SUPPER. she has accumulated tons of knowledge in the last 100 pages of experience. Annie's good advice and coaching and Fenmarian's sweet attitude and the Author's IBM helped immeasurably.

Brett and Jacob stop talking. everything's been said.

they hug like two delicate, caring fleas. they wrap their gentle arms around each other. in silence they feel fear and love swarm up into their throats and bloodstreams. the combinations of emotion mixing inside them cause heart palpitations, stomach butterflies and weak knees. they are growing up. is it worth it? they think so. they seem to have no other choice at present. they are facing their lives squarely in the face. they are facing each other round in the face. they are stuck together in the historical and geometric inclinations of their fates and faces. well, anyway, they *are* linked in a familiar embrace.

Is Jacob really changing? is Brett really changed? it's very possible. everyone does change, you know, a little from time to time. OH. AND ISN'T IT PRETTY TO THINK SO!

73 JACOB HAS CIRCLED the block three times clockwise and three times counter-clockwise, mustering up the courage to enter the Main Library's front door and weave his way back to the stacks. now he has reached his destination. now a sinking feeling in his gut tells him: i wish i hadn't found her.

But it's too late, baby. there she is staring back at him, surprised and disgusted.

Annie: what are *you* doing here?

Jacob: i came to see you.

Jacob and Annie are whispering in the Library. the last place left in the Universe where Annie feels safe and undisturbed has been invaded, and by the enemy no less. no wonder she's disturbed. she thinks: he's got his nerve! while he's thinking: my nerves are shot.

Annie: i'm very busy, Jacob.

Jacob: i know that, Annie. i'm sorry. it wasn't easy to come. could i have just a minute or two?

Student: hey pipe down, will ya?!

Annie cares about preserving her reputation at the Library. you don't maintain good standing among Library People by informally chatting with conspicuous, loud Men in dirty overalls. Jacob is drawing attention from Annie's cohorts, so she agrees to go outside and sit on the ledge with Jacob in order to safeguard her academic image. while they approach the outdoors, Annie is thinking: doesn't he ever take those overalls off? Jacob is thinking: this isn't going to be easy. i wish i'd left before i got here.

They sit down on the ledge beside the bright daisies. Jacob immediately picks one and twirls it between his jittery fingers. Annie holds a pencil between her angry fingers. she speaks first.

Annie: o.k., shoot. what is it?

Jacob (taking a deep breath for control; he blurts it out anyway): I KNOW YOU HATE ME, Annie. i know you can't stand my relationship with Brett. and i know i haven't been so nice to you . . .

Annie (annoyed): come on, Jacob. we both know we don't have a lot to say to each other. you're here for a reason. get to the point.

Jacob: Brett really cares about you (pause). she says you're good for her (pause). apparently the crazy things that happen between us don't happen between you (pause).

Annie: yeah. true so far.

Jacob: i really want to work things out with Brett. and she does with me, Annie! couldn't you and i work out a peaceful co-existence? i mean looks like we're going to be in each other's lives for awhile anyway?!

Annie (blankly): how so, Jacob?

Jacob (uncomfortable): don't be so tough on me, Annie. i'm just trying to get along. we're bound to run into each other. i'm tired of fighting and avoiding you. i'm tired of fighting with Brett/women/everybody. (Jacob looks sincere. maybe he's mellowing with age? at twenty-eight? it's possible. maybe he's just more frightened.)

Annie: your words are great. really! i'm beginning to see why Brett returns to the scene of the crime over and over again; good lines and a great delivery!

Jacob smiles charmingly at Annie, taking this as a compliment. quickly he is embarrassed, realizing his moustache and blue eyes are up to their old tricks again, twitching and winking and flirting with Annie, which is not why he came/this time/believe it or not.

Jacob: i know i've got a lot of work to do. i'm trying to do it with myself and in my Men's Group—like you suggested, remember Annie? but some of my process goes on between Brett and me. i'd really appreciate it if you weren't always turning her against me.

Annie (her eyes alight with recognition): ah ah! the truth reveals itself! now i get the friendly visit. you don't really give a damn whether we understand each other or really get along; you just don't want to lose.

Jacob (wanting to change the drift of conversation): can't we start over? can't we be CIVIL?

Annie: seems to me you're pretty barbarian most of the time. i bet you'd love it if the Author got rid of women like me. life would be easier for you and the boys, wouldn't it? but you're not going to see that happen, not in this novel or the next, or the next! I'M REALLY HERE. me and other women like myself. and WE'RE MULTIPLYING, JACOB. (Annie makes a goblin's face at him to indicate scary, dangerous monsters on the loose.) neither you or any Author can stop us now with Big Erasers or Big Mouths.

Jacob: i know. i know that now . . .

Annie: and you're not going to get me in bed with those sneaky blue eyes. i'm immune to you.

Jacob: you act like i'm some kind of disease!

Annie: for me, you are. getting too close to you would give me a rash; i'm sure of it.

Jacob: well, i'm not asking for that, Annie. i just want to be friends. i admit it though . . . the thought had entered my mind. i wanted to . . . even thought i could get to you. then i realized you really weren't interested and i felt rejected. it was a blow to my ego, for sure.

Annie: nice of you to admit it. but, of course, i knew.

Jacob (astounded): you did? how?

Annie: you think you're so mystifying? hey, pal, your motives come singing through loud and clear as a bell.

ding! dong! simple as kindergarten. i've watched your type for years. even got a few rashes in my day. i know when a man is trapped in his pants.

Jacob (embarrassed by Annie's frankness): well...

Annie: anyway, even if we got along, it's really irrelevant, you know. i'm not hungry for anything from you. so i'm safe. i don't need you. my sexuality is more directed to...

Jacob (interrupting): yeah. well i thought so. i mean i guess i better get going...

Annie (slowly and succinctly): WOMEN. hard to hear, is it? (she is amused at how easily she overpowers and intimidates Jacob; how thin the skin of MACHO HEROES!)

Jacob (giving in): honestly, yes. it's threatening to me. especially because of Brett.

Annie: i get that. (noting his vulnerability, Annie softens.) i'm still concerned about Brett's hunger for you, though lately it seems she's learning to feed herself.

Jacob: yeah. you can say that again! it's me who's the real wreck now. in comparison she's the strong one, and she's so busy i hardly get to see her.

Annie: i appreciate your coming by, Jacob, and trying to be honest with me. i'm not on any warpath. i have better things to do with my time than plot against you. i'm just staying alert to protect and defend myself and the women i love.

Jacob: i can see that. (half to himself): shit, sometimes i wish i had a male friend i could really talk to, like you and Brett.

Annie: you do have Fenmarian and Tuna Melitta. they seem awfully nice, and very sensitive. i imagine they'd be great friends.

Jacob: oh yeah. they are, but they're not Men. they're just a flea and a cat; they're just Animals.

Annie: animals are a beginning.

Jacob: i suppose. yes. things are looking up! Brett and i are getting along and communicating better than ever! (he looks to Annie for reassurance, but doesn't get the expected nods. Annie says nothing and doesn't budge her head.)

Jacob: we're trying harder!

Annie: again?

Jacob: yeah again. and again. i'm a fighter, Annie.

Annie: so am i. so is Brett!

Jacob (sincerely): you're a very strong woman. and very beautiful. it's scary to me and yet, well i think it's wonderful. i think as i overcome insecurities in myself about control and ego stuff, i'm going to appreciate independent women a lot more.

Jacob says this from his heart instead of his gonads. it affects his recently active tear ducts. they are filling up and spilling over; it's an endless waterfall coming from a dry-eyed wonder boy. pretty strange, huh? quite a different fellow lately. he certainly has vastly different responses coming from his involuntary nervous system. besides crying, he's sweating buckets of water underneath his overalls and shaking bundles of nerves underneath his skin.

Annie (cooly but pleasantly): thanks, Jacob. i wish you luck.

Jacob: well, listen. i'll let you get back to work. (trying to pull himself together, he straightens up and smooths his hair for something to do. then he changes the subject.) sooooo! how is the thesis coming along?

Annie: great. can't complain. seems you ought to get back to work, too, huh Jacob? you've got centuries to cover.

They smile. they shake hands. an unknown feeling enters Jacob's chest and shoots to his brain, while he is holding this woman's hand. it is a sense of EQUALITY. he thoroughly enjoys holding this warm, strong, female hand.

Annie lets go first and moves on. they walk towards their own work/research/lives. Jacob still feels the essence of that extraordinary hand in his. and the beat of it goes on and on. somehow he knows that shaking it has affected his life forever. even if he chooses to deny it later, he knows presently that he's met a woman who is stronger than he in so many vital and unimagined ways.

74 FENMARIAN HAS CALLED a meeting of the characters in the basement. she looks great. she's been resting up lately. she'd been working too hard trying to feed everyone. all the needy, hungry people in the novel, where do they all come from? Fen's been making too many salads and doing too much therapy for all of them. after her near fatal accident, i instructed her to take a lot of naps. wow! what a world of good it's done her!

WELCOME BACK, FEN! she wants to discuss the future of this novel. Jacob couldn't make this important meeting because of his odd job at the radio station. he's playing Country Western music today. why? i haven't the slightest idea. i guess that's his job. i never told him to do that. i know nothing whatsoever about country western music.

Everyone else is in attendance at this novel meeting. Brett, alternately listening and tuning out to write in her diary. Tuna Melitta who's sitting on my lap. yes, i'm there too; Annie, sitting skeptically against the wall with her sunglasses and trench coat, paying close attention and taking notes of her own. WALKING VANILLA is floating in the air.

Fenmarian: i wish Jacob were here but i can understand his need to make money. we all can. i thought we'd get together and help the Author out, since she's not sure about how to end this novel.

Author (defensive): I DON'T NEED HELP, Fenmarian.

Fenmarian: now. now. don't get all excited, we know that, Susan.

Annie: right on for saying it, Susan.

Brett (looking up from her diary): right on. i think you're doing great, Susan. you've helped me immensely.

you can end this novel anyway you want. i think i can make it from here.

Author: thanks, Annie. thanks, Brett. well now. (regaining her self-confidence, clearing her throat, she goes on in a louder, more professionally confident tone): THIS HAS BEEN THE HOLIDAYS. there are a number of people who think they have nowhere to go. they go off bridges. sometimes, off edges. suicide is most popular during the holidays when everyone is having a BALL drinking and eating and kissing each other to death. it's odd but true. it's a statistic so it's got to be true. statistics are always true. so are paintings/poems and my characters. facts are facts, SO THERE!

THE CAUSE: 1977

THE RESULT: 1978

Take it or leave it.

. . .

With my imagination, i have manipulated these characters; they haven't minded. it's given them something to do. sometimes when Brett had her period and was especially irritable, i rubbed her shoulders and back, gave her B vitamins and calcium tablets. i took care of my characters. i even loaned Jacob money for a new battery. i gave aid to my needy characters. who else would?

i had them go out to dinner two or three nights a week. they both really loved that. i like seeing them enjoy themselves. i get vicarious pleasure from perfectly happy characters. i let them splurge a few times — remember the pork chops? remember the champagne? i even sent them to the movies several evenings when they couldn't actually afford to go. they loved that too. all and all, they had a pretty good time. my characters haven't minded the things i made them do because they know deep down inside the novel, i have meant well.

. . .

This has been the story of a relationship that lasts all the way from tuesday until friday, only three days, yet

134

goes on for three months, three years or forever in different forms/faces/voices and hands. the story of Brett and
Jacob, who dated briefly, for three days but go on and on
in different ways/clothes/cities/and languages. the story
that happens to everybody. the story that goes on and on
and on.

The story of WALKING VANILLA. the story of
struggles up a very funny, odd ladder towards awareness/
success/happiness. the story of characters coming together as a POLITICAL ACT. loving your friends and
lovers and treating them well *is* a political act; do your
honest best.

My characters will be forever HUNGRY. they will
run. they will rest. they will vegetate. they will stare at
walls. Jacob with grease on his face and a cat on his lap
and tools in his hand. Brett with inspiration in her mind
and croissants in her mouth. Annie with a Thesis on the
desk and M and M's in her purse. it is necessary once in
awhile to get lost/to get stuck/inside. it gives perspective.
depth of soul. it takes us to the delicious heart of the
matter.

Brett is slim and so is Jacob. they may grow old and
fat. they are getting along now on new, modern terms.
it may last and it may not. they are trying their honest
best. so am i. i get bogged down as you can tell if you are
reading carefully; you can see mistakes. i'll leave them in
as evidence of imperfection. let's celebrate our imperfection instead of condemning it; it's what makes the
human race adorable in its own particular, baboon
fashion. now, i'm going to give my characters a chance
to say goodbye for themselves. it's the only DEMOCRAT-
IC WAY TO GO. Jacob, say goodbye to the readers.

Jacob: goodbye! see you real soon! i'd like to add a
note for the men out there. the Author's right, fellas.
feelings are good for you, even if they make you shake
and scare you to death, they won't kill you! they start
feeling pretty nice, in fact, after awhile. give it a whirl.
pay attention. i did, and i'm glad.

Annie: there *is* friendship. there is good work for

women beyond HOUSEWORK. there are lovely poems and paintings and music and friends that invade each other with joy/laughter/grapefruits/sunlight and love.

Brett: on the kitchen floor/at Brennan's/in the Park/ in the great outdoors/and indoors/windows and hearts/ there is love.

Author: Wow! our characters can be terribly tender when they make an effort. when they PAY ATTENTION. when they TRUST. they can WALK WITH VANILLA when they have faith. Brett and Jacob and Annie and Buddy and Fen have improved vastly inside even if you may not see it OUT THERE. it's true. it's authentic. they do love each other better now that they have almost lost each other. we do learn (a little) from our: mistakes/tragedies/ time/schools/parents/friends/lovers and houseplants.

Annie: have a ball with your friends. have POT LUCK SUPPERS with your closest pals. it will help change things faster. IT WILL TASTE GOOD.

75 Buddy: so who wrote this novel?
Author: Susan Efros wrote this novel, and the Collective Unconscious, and it's a pretty good novel, not great, but pretty good.

When the novel ends, life goes on. usually. we go on. hopefully. keep PRACTICING. PRACTICE MAKES ALMOST PERFECT.

LOVE,

SUSAN

76 FENMARIAN HAS ENTERED the Author's helicopter. THE NOVEL SHIFTS DIRECTION. Fenmarian is above the Author now, looking down from the clear blue sky. wonderful, whirling Fenmarian watching the Author enter a cafe and order a glass of French white burgundy wine. the novelist has just finished writing her book and is celebrating with a glass of high class alcohol. she needs it; she admits it. she doesn't hide her neurosis, not anymore! she is comfortably imperfect, just like you are.

. . .

Fenmarian is prepared to take off with a large bag of fresh vegetables and the entire crew. Fenmarian is going to travel around the world making large, green salads because that's what she-he likes to do best.

Fen watches the Author from above. Fen knows that the Author is hungry and that her back hurts. Fen knows that everyone is hungry and most people's backs hurt. the Author does not know that Fen is watching from the helicopter in the sky; she isn't paying attention to the sky presently.

Buddy: if Fenmarian is such a wonderful flea, why is she stealing the Author's helicopter? after all the Author has done for her!

Jacob: beats me.

Buddy: hi ya, Jacob. you know, you've been saying a lot of nice things lately.

Jacob: thanks, Buddy. i'm surprised. i thought you were too preoccupied with money and success and business luncheons to hear anything.

Buddy: not true, young man. (offended): i've heard a great deal, actually. more than you'd imagine. you underestimate me, Jacob.

Jacob: that's very possible.

Buddy: i think you're pretty nice, Jake.

Jacob: hey, is that your shotgun?

Buddy: well, yes it is. but don't get me wrong. i never use it. it's strictly for self-protection, in tunnels and other danger zones.

Jacob: i see. hey, the Author's been mad at you a lot, huh?

Buddy: oh i don't mind.

Jacob: i guess you wouldn't.

Buddy: this book is going to be a bestseller.

Jacob: that's nice.

Buddy: you're pretty close with Fenmarian, aren't you?

Jacob: oh yes. very!

Buddy: so i guess you approve of her stealing the helicopter?

Jacob: i haven't thought about it.

Buddy: you may be a very famous character someday, young man.

Jacob: i don't mind. personally, i think Fenmarian is going to be the memorable character in this novel, and nobody deserves the recognition more.

Buddy: you're a good friend, Jacob. i envy you for your friends.

Jacob: you can have them too, Buddy. you just have to take risks, WALK WITH VANILLA, things like that.

Buddy: yes, i know. i mean i've heard. i'm trying in my own way.

Jacob: i'm sure you are.

Buddy: so tell me, Jake. where is that wonderful girlfriend of yours, Brett?

Jacob: she's in the helicopter too; but don't call her my girlfriend. that's not what this novel's about.

Buddy: oh yes. i forgot. she's a person, right? i'm so sorry.

Jacob: that's o.k., Buddy. i'm just learning myself.

Buddy: it's commendable, your growth in the novel, Jake.

Jacob: as you can see, i'm forced to change. otherwise i'd lose Brett, for sure, and probably a lot more. my growth is a survival tool.

Buddy: your adaptation to tools is very high. i admire that.

Jacob: i was brought up that way. it's the only way i know. unfortunately, sometimes i'm more comfortable with a wrench than a person, but i'm trying to overcome that too.

Buddy: what do you think of that Annie? she's a feisty one, huh?

Jacob: we don't get along so well, that's true. but she makes some good points and she's smart, that's for sure! i think she's too hard on Men, but she says Men have always been too hard on Women. i'm tired of fighting with her, so i'm going to try harder to get along, even if we don't see eye to eye. i guess she's a pretty o.k. lady.

Buddy: you don't like me, though, do you, Jacob? you can be honest with me.

Jacob: it's not that simple, Buddy. i've been brainwashed against professionals like you. maybe you remind me of my father or an uncle, who knows? anyway, it's nothing personal; it's just my early childhood training acting up.

Buddy (taking advantage of this generous moment): hey, is it true that you slept with the Author? (an excited gleam appears in Buddy's eyes.)

Jacob: hey, come on, Buddy! don't ask me things like that. ask her if you want to know. and besides, it's none of your fucking business.

Buddy (frowning): i was afraid you were going to say that, damn!

Jacob (smiling sheepishly): hey, Buddy, have *you* slept with the Author?

Buddy (insulted): my word, of course not. my God. i'm a happily married man! besides my relationship to the Author is purely professional.

Jacob: i see.

Buddy: well, i'm glad you do. (calming down, wiping his forehead with a handkerchief, straightening his tie, clearing his throat): well, it seems all the characters except you are in the helicopter?

Jacob: yes, that's true. but they're coming to get me soon. i just got off work at the radio station. they'll be here to pick me up any minute now. (an idea comes to Jacob): hey, Buddy, would you like to come along? might do you a world of good!

Buddy (flattered and scared): um, where are you going?

Jacob: we're going to be in another novel.

Buddy: why are you going to do that?

Jacob: because ALL MY FRIENDS ARE GOING, AND I WANT TO BE WITH THEM.

Buddy: what's it about? this new novel you're involved in?

Jacob: i have no idea. but Susan's up there. she'll tell us.

Buddy (incredulous): you're going anyway without knowing your part?

Jacob: sure, why not? it's an experience. NEVER UNDERESTIMATE THE VALUE OF BEING WITH FRIENDS AND HAVING NEW EXPERIENCES. are you going to come?

Buddy: thanks. but no. i think i'll stay here.

Jacob: and do what?

Buddy: oh, you know, make money. things like that. i'll keep busy.

Jacob (smiling affectionately): goodbye, Buddy. i hope you make some friends this year!

Buddy (smiling back, more openly than he ever has): thanks, Jacob. i hope so too!

. . .

The helicopter descends. Fenmarian reaches out her little flea hands and hoists Jacob up into the plane. a few leaves of fresh spinach fall from the helicopter as the Author and her characters disappear into the powder blue sky.